JEWISH BIOGRAPHY SERIES

I LIFT MY LAMP

EMMA LAZARUS
AND THE
STATUE OF LIBERTY

NANCY SMILER LEVINSON

illustrated with photographs

*To the Readers of the
Ashland Public Library*

Best wishes,

Nancy Smiler Levinson

LODESTAR BOOKS E. P. Dutton New York

Library of Congress Cataloging in Publication Data

Levinson, Nancy Smiler.
   I lift my lamp.

   (Jewish biography series)
   "Lodestar books."
   Summary: A biography of the American poet, activist for humane causes, and friend to immigrants, who authored the noble words now inscribed on the Statue of Liberty.
   1. Lazarus, Emma, 1849-1887—Juvenile literature.
2. Statue of Liberty (New York, N.Y.)—Juvenile literature.   3. Poets, American—19th century—Biography—Juvenile literature.   4. Jews—New York (N.Y.)—Biography—Juvenile literature.   [1. Lazarus, Emma, 1849-1887.   2. Poets, American.   3. Jews—Biography.   4. Statue of Liberty (New York, N.Y.)]
I. Title.   II. Series.
PS2234.L48   1986   811'.4 [B] [92]   86-4394
ISBN 0-525-67180-3

Published in the United States by E. P. Dutton, 2 Park Avenue, New York, N.Y. 10016

Published simultaneously in Canada by Fitzhenry & Whiteside Limited, Toronto

Editor: Virginia Buckley

Printed in the U.S.A.   W   First Edition

10 9 8 7 6 5 4 3 2 1

for my mother and father
and sisters, Gail and Maurine

Acknowledgments

For their assistance with my research and for their encouragement and support, I wish to acknowledge Joanne Rocklin; Rosemary Brosnan; Ruth Cohen; Morris U. Schappes; University of Judaism, Los Angeles; Helen Rogaway; Emily Nathan; David Benjamin Starr, American Jewish Historical Society; Rabbi Theodore Lewis, Touro Synagogue; Los Angeles Public Library; Dr. Stanley Chyet, Hebrew Union College, Los Angeles; Jewish Federation Council of Greater Los Angeles; Oliver Orr, Jr., Library of Congress; Linda Thal and Roz Kane, Leo Baeck Synagogue; Michael Cart, Marilynn Saunders, Elena Panajotovic, Frank Piontek, Agnes Song, Meri-Martha Wascsepinecz, Jeff Falco, Chris Olson, and the entire staff of the Beverly Hills Public Library; my husband, Irwin; and my sons, Matt and Daniel.

Rabbis Sanford Ragins and Leonard Beerman have inspired me.

I also wish to express special thanks to Virginia Buckley.

Contents

1
Mighty Woman with a Torch

A dense, misty fog hovered over New York Harbor, but the officials on Bedloe's Island refused to let the gloomy weather interfere with their ceremony. No matter that the Statue of Liberty, still partly veiled, could barely be seen in the fog. The enormous monument had been in the making for fifteen years, and a great many people had long awaited this momentous occasion.

The statue was a gift to the United States from France, which so admired American democracy and wished to seal the friendship between the two countries. France had helped America win its fight for independence from England a century earlier, and America had become a shining example of liberty to the world. Many Frenchmen had tired of wars and revolutions and leadership by despotic emperors in their own country. By presenting a gift symbolizing liberty, they also hoped to give a message to their rulers, expressing their own desire for democracy.

One of those hopeful Frenchmen was a renowned sculptor named Frédéric Auguste Bartholdi. He had enthusiastically accepted the idea of building such a statue when it was suggested by a friend. Auguste always favored massive statuary, but this would be greater than anything he had ever done. The agreement between the two countries had held that France would build the statue, while America would erect the pedestal large enough and grand enough to support it.

After so many years of work, faced with more hurdles than he cared to recall, Auguste had finally accomplished his mission.

Now on this day, October 28, 1886, the handsome, bearded sculptor joined the throngs of people gathering for the dedication ceremony. First the officials, the bands and armed forces units, the groups of schoolchildren, and the numerous patriotic societies—numbering twenty thousand people in all—made their way along a five-mile parade route in lower New York City. The parade took so long, the lunch planned for the officials had to be canceled.

Then, at last, the American and French dignitaries embarked in boats that took them from the Battery across to the tiny island. Immediately harbor festivities began with a display of three hundred water vessels and the sounds of booming cannons and shrill steam whistles. Bands played "Hail Columbia," "Yankee Doodle," and the French national anthem, "La Marseillaise."

The dignitaries, including President Grover Cleveland, and even several French citizens from Auguste's distant hometown of Colmar, stepped onto the platform that had been constructed especially for the ceremony.

Auguste took a different place, however. He climbed up three hundred feet above the crowd and perched himself in the torch that Miss Liberty majestically held high overhead. There he grasped a rope tied to a three-colored sheet that was draped over the top of the statue. He was to await a

Dedication ceremony for the Statue of Liberty, October 28, 1886 NATIONAL PARK SERVICE: STATUE OF LIBERTY NATIONAL MONUMENT

signal from a teenage boy selected to let Auguste know when to pull the rope for the unveiling.

The first speaker was a clergyman, who read a prayer. He was followed by several more speakers. Then Senator William M. Evarts, a former secretary of state, stood to say a few well-chosen words. But when he paused in the middle to take a breath, the young boy mistook the pause for the end of his speech. Quickly and eagerly he signaled up to the torch. On cue, Auguste yanked the rope, and the large sheet fell away. There, at last, stood the magnificent copper monument—the woman holding the torch in her right hand and the Declaration of Independence in the other—entitled by the sculptor, Liberty Enlightening the World.

The cheers and shouts, flag waving, and hat tossing at the sight of such an extraordinary work of art were so exuberant that Senator Evarts gave up trying to finish his speech. All he could do was return to his chair. The excitement and clamor continued for such a long time that President Cleveland's words officially accepting the gift on behalf of the American people were barely audible. Yet, he spoke: "We will not forget that Liberty has made here her home, nor shall her chosen altar be neglected . . . a stream of light shall pierce the darkness of ignorance and man's oppression until Liberty enlightens the world."

By then it had begun to drizzle, causing the fireworks display to be postponed until another day. At five o'clock the crowd dispersed to find shelter from the rain and to hurry home and dress for a scheduled banquet.

The list of those who had been invited to the ceremony was lengthy. Of course, many important people were overlooked. But there was one person in particular who was missing that day. Her name was Emma Lazarus.

There was more than one reason Emma was not there to celebrate. First, women were never included in such affairs. Only two were present, Auguste's wife, Jeanne-Emilie, and the wife of one American official. The explanation given was that women might be hurt in the rush of the crowd. Many women were fighting for equal rights at the time, and the suffrage movement calling for the right of women to vote was growing stronger year by year, but it was still a world controlled by men.

Another reason Emma was not invited was that she did not figure importantly in the story of the Statue of Liberty at the time of its unveiling.

That was not to come until later. True, she had written a sonnet about the statue in which she referred to it as "Mother of Exiles." To her it was a symbol welcoming weary immigrants to a country that would allow them to live and worship freely. Her sonnet was entitled "The New Colossus," and it had been written three years earlier, at the urging of

Senator Evarts, for an auction to raise money for the pedestal building fund. But "The New Colossus" was printed in a portfolio with other contributors' works, sold to the highest bidder, and forgotten for the time being.

No one at the auction or the dedication ceremony could know the fate of Emma Lazarus's inspired work, but her words were to become immortal and would stir the hearts of all who read them, whether born on American soil or recently come with hopes and dreams to the promised golden land.

No one knew then that part of her verse would be engraved on a plaque to be placed inside the statue's pedestal.

> "Give me your tired, your poor,
> Your huddled masses yearning to breathe free,
> The wretched refuse of your teeming shore.
> Send these, the homeless, tempest-tost to me,
> I lift my lamp beside the golden door!"

But once these words were emblazoned for all to read, they were to give a deeper and more significant meaning to the statue than it had at the start. Not only did the statue celebrate the ideal of liberty, but it became the world's greatest symbol of freedom and hope. For immigrants, Miss Liberty was their first sight of the new land.

During her lifetime Emma, too, was to grow and change, to become a more deeply fulfilled and enriched person than she imagined possible. Even though she was not an exile from another country, she had traveled a long road. Like the woman with the torch, Emma held her own lamp in hand while searching along the path that ultimately led her to become a poet, a humanist, and a patriot.

2
Young Emma's World

Emma Lazarus grew up privileged and sheltered. It seemed unlikely that a girl in her position would someday come to be concerned with people from a world far removed from hers.

Emma was born July 22, 1849, into a wealthy, upper-class home in a fashionable New York City district. She was a proper girl of the nineteenth century, a time when females were protected by the menfolk. Women were held by men to be delicate and even weak-minded, fit only to bear children and take care of the home. It was not acceptable for women to speak in public or write anything other than letters, or perhaps poetry, to be read only by the family.

Laws, too, kept women downtrodden as citizens. In most states women were not legally entitled to own property. In fact, if a woman inherited any property, whether a parcel of land or merely a necklace, upon marriage it legally became her husband's. If he wanted, he could use it to pay off a business or gambling debt.

The state of New York was becoming the center of a new movement, one that was speaking out for women's rights. Leaders like Elizabeth Cady Stanton and Susan B. Anthony were holding conventions, speaking and writing and working toward changing some of the unjust laws. It was a painful battle for these women, though. They were in ever-present danger, stoned or spat upon, called amazons and sour old maids in the newspapers, and even threatened with death.

Emma's world was confined to her family and their brownstone house on West Fourteenth Street. It was not the Fifth Avenue millionaire's row, but the neighborhood had an aristocratic air of its own. The houses were furnished with the finest carpeting and curtains and splendid, ornately carved furniture stuffed with plush cushions. The fabric covering was made of imported silks or brocades. Emma's home also had a large and beautiful piano in the parlor.

Residents took great care with their dress. Men wore top hats and carried canes. Women strolled the cobblestone streets wearing long dresses filled out with stiff crinoline material worn underneath, a lace or cashmere shawl around their shoulders, and a bonnet to match each costume. Never would a lady venture out for tea or set foot in a carriage to ride in Central Park without carrying a lace handkerchief.

As Emma was growing up in these lovely and quiet surroundings, she knew little of the bitter battle for women's rights. She knew little of the cruel institution of slavery in America and the movement to abolish it. She knew little of the poor and needy in other New York neighborhoods and the many reform movements underway to help them.

During those years, in the 1850s, New York City's population was steadily increasing. There were just more than half a million people, and about half of those citizens had been born elsewhere, either in other parts of America or in countries like Ireland, Germany, England, or France, from where many had escaped revolutions or economic hardship. Certainly with such diverse cultural and religious differences, there were bound to be clashes, but for the most part people lived and worked peacefully together in New York's melting pot.

The Lazarus family was Jewish. In the city, the Jewish population numbered 10,000, one-fifth of the Semitic population of the country. Neither Emma nor her family experienced anti-Semitism. It did not exist overtly the way it did in many European countries. So Emma was then unaware of the part of Jewish history that saw persecution of its people century after century. She had no reason to know that in many other places Jews were denied fundamental rights and often ridiculed and treated harshly as well.

Emma lived in a secure and genteel world with her father, Moses, and mother, Esther; her older sisters, Josephine, Sarah, and Mary; her brother, Eleazer Frank; and younger sisters, Agnes and Annie. Two other boys had died at birth, sad and distressful events for Mr. and Mrs. Lazarus, who were disappointed at losing sons. Sons carried on the family name and tradition, especially in a Jewish household. Sons were important in a male-dominated world.

But the Lazarus family could count its blessings. They had seven children, a luxuriously comfortable home with hired domestic help, and relatively few worries. They even had the privilege of being able to leave the heat and hustle of city life each summer for several weeks at a seaside home, The Beeches, in Newport, Rhode Island.

Emma's father, Moses, had become prosperous in the sugar-refining business, a process of purifying sugarcane into white crystals. The cane was raised in the hot climate of Louisiana, a long way from New York, but Moses Lazarus seemed to have no trouble managing his business from afar.

In fact, it was on rare occasions that he left his family, which was an extraordinarily close one. A visitor was amazed to see how strongly attached they were to one another. The visitor, Thomas Wentworth Higginson, an abolitionist, writer, and high-ranking army officer, remarked to a friend, "I chanced to call at the house, and found everyone there in such distress that I thought something terrible must have occurred. My hasty inquiry of the daughters brought out the fact that their father was going away: But, I asked, he will come back? 'Yes, tomorrow night,' was the mournful reply."

Moses Lazarus had a strong, binding hold over his family, yet he was also affectionate and loving. A cultured, well-read, and refined man, he took an active role in important New York social clubs. Emma's mother, Esther, who was called Hettie, was occupied running the household and caring for the children.

Both Emma's parents had backgrounds that were rich in culture and history and that included ancestors who contributed in important ways to their Jewish communities and to the larger society around them.

Emma's maternal ancestors came from Germany around the beginning of the 1700s and were referred to as "*Ashkenazim*," the Hebrew word for Germany. Her paternal ancestors were Spanish Sephardim and had journeyed to the new land decades earlier. When the Ashkenazim arrived, they were looked down upon by the Sephardim, who considered themselves more elite.

But by the time Hettie Nathan and Moses Lazarus were married in 1840, the Ashkenazim and Sephardim had resolved their differences and had come to live and worship together.

In Hettie's family there were a number of prominent people. One of the earliest known was a rabbi named Gershom Mendez Seixas, who led his congregation at the Shearith Israel Synagogue in New York City at the time of the American Revolution. He was an ardent patriot, throwing his full support to the American cause. When the British redcoats captured New York City, Gershom Mendez Seixas urged his congregation to leave the city. He was convinced that staying under British rule would be the same as collaborating with the enemy. Some members chose not to leave, but the majority joined him in self-imposed exile in Connecticut and Pennsylvania for the duration of the war.

When the newly independent nation was meeting to draw up its constitution, there was both a new democratic spirit throughout the land and a renewed spirit of religious freedom.

Also on her maternal side Emma had an uncle, J. J. Lyons, who during her lifetime was the *hazan,* the cantor or reader, who led the services at Shearith Israel. Concerned not only with helping the Jews of his community, J. J. Lyons believed it was important to reach out in all directions. While a potato famine in Ireland was causing the Irish to starve and many to emigrate to America, he delivered an impassioned speech from his pulpit, appealing for aid in their behalf.

Another uncle, Albert C. Cardozo, was a justice on the New York State Supreme Court, and his son Benjamin served as a justice on the United States Supreme Court in Washington, D.C. Hettie's brother Benjamin Nathan was a banker and a member of the New York Stock Exchange.

The story of Emma's paternal ancestors dates back to a period known as the Golden Age in Spain. Sephardic is the Hebrew name for Spain, and there Jews had lived and flourished for a long time—that was until the year 1478.

That time was historically important in Europe for the institution of the Spanish Inquisition, which persecuted Jews throughout Spain. Jews were offered a choice. Either they could convert to Catholicism or they would be forced to leave the land. Many converted, but of those, a good number outwardly pretended to be Christians yet continued to practice Judaism in secret. They became known as *Marranos,* a Spanish word for *pigs* or *swine.* Others refused outright to convert and were mercilessly tortured until they changed their minds or perished.

In 1492, the same year King Ferdinand and Queen Isabella sent Columbus to sea, they issued a new edict, expelling the Jews. Many fled. Thousands went to Portugal, but within a few years, the Portuguese crown put a stop to the flow of newcomers by charging a high fee of anyone wishing to remain there. As a result, the Jews were forced to move on further. They turned to new routes, ones that led them to Turkey, North Africa, Italy, France, Holland, and South America. Eventually a few sailed westward to the New World.

In 1654, twenty-three people, including six men, four women, and thirteen children, seeking a homeland where they could live and work and bring up their families in peace, sailed in a French frigate to New York, which then was a Dutch colony called New Amsterdam.

The small, courageous group, which set out from Brazil, was led by a young father named Asser Levy van Swellem. He refused to have his children grow up in fear of further inquisitions. Travel in those days was difficult enough, but to make the journey worse, their ship was caught in a storm and captured by a band of Spanish pirates. Amazingly the travelers were rescued, and the ship that helped them escape sent them on their way.

It was in September, shortly before Rosh Hashanah, the Jewish New Year, that they arrived in New Amsterdam. Eagerly they started to step ashore and accept the welcome by Governor Peter Stuyvesant, who had come down to the harbor. But they were not welcomed.

The Dutch governor refused permission for them to disembark and set foot on the soil. Peter Stuyvesant immediately wrote his superiors in Holland that Jews were "deceitful" and he did not want them to "infect and trouble this new colony." For him, there was only one religion, the Dutch Reformed Church, and anyone of a different belief was suspicious.

Furious, Levy told the governor of their long, harrowing

journey. They had no intention of turning around and going back, he insisted. They would refuse to budge. If they had to sit in the harbor all winter, Levy said, they would do just that!

That did not make Peter Stuyvesant change his mind, and although he did not welcome the newcomers, he didn't want to be responsible for letting them starve or freeze to death. So, throughout the winter, the Jews were temporarily housed and cared for by the Dutch Reformed Church welfare funds.

Finally, urged by his Dutch authorities to permit the Jews entry, Stuyvesant consented and granted them the right to stay. The first Jews of America had landed.

Levy and his friends, their children and grandchildren, however, had to fight for many of their basic rights. For a long time they were allowed neither to own real estate nor to travel and trade freely like their Gentile neighbors. But eventually they became good merchants and craftsmen, and were well respected in their communities. During the American Revolution, understanding the treasure of freedom, most stood strongly behind America's cause in its fight for independence from England.

The twenty-three Jews who had journeyed to the New World viewed themselves as remnants of Israel, a distant land of the past, and when they established the country's first synagogue, they named it Shearith Israel, "remnant of Israel." It remained the only synagogue in New York from 1655 until 1825—nearly two hundred years.

The small wood-frame building they rented served as a house of worship as well as a community center. Later the congregation was able to buy a building of its own, and in time Shearith Israel came to be known as the Spanish and Portuguese Synagogue. Today it still stands, located at West Seventieth Street in New York City, and some of Emma's family's descendants worship there among the congregation.

It was this Sephardic lineage dating back to the seventeenth-century ocean journey that Emma's father could boast as his ancestral background. And it was Shearith Israel Synagogue that the Lazarus family attended on important Jewish occasions. They were not actively involved in a great many synagogue affairs, but they observed Jewish customs, honored the Sabbath, and celebrated the holidays of the year. Always at the Passover dinner, Eleazer Frank, the only son, read the portion of the traditional seder service that was designated for the younger son of a Jewish family.

Emma certainly participated in these rituals, but she was to admit that in her youth she was not stirred by inner religious fervor.

In the Lazarus household, both Emma's parents put strong emphasis on refinement, culture, and education. Emma's father did not believe, as many men did, that females would fall ill with a fever from too much mental activity. He saw to it that his daughters, as well as his son, were tutored at home, a common method for educating the upper class. For girls, there were few schools beyond the elementary level anyway. The Lazarus youngsters studied literature, arithmetic, history, geography, music, and languages. Emma played the piano and grew to be especially fond of the compositions of Robert Schumann and Frédéric Chopin. She also became remarkably proficient in not one foreign language but three—French, German, and Italian.

Emma hardly had to be persuaded to study. It was clear from early childhood that the little girl with the dark hair and deep, dark eyes was gifted. So easily and with such passion did she take to literature and poetry that when she began to write her first poems, her talent was recognized immediately by her family. They called her poems songs and Emma herself a born singer.

Studying as often as she did, Emma had little time for play. Sometimes, though, she allowed herself amusement with dolls, except she didn't give them family roles in the traditional game of playing house. Rather, she named them after

Greek or Roman mythological gods and goddesses, heroes and heroines. Or she called them by such names as Guinevere or Sir Lancelot, characters from King Arthur's court.

Sensitive songstress that she was at home, outwardly Emma was shy and self-conscious. She simply found it easier to write than to speak. Her older sister Josephine said, "Books were her world from her earliest years. In them she literally lost and found herself."

3
A Monumental Idea

While young Emma took for granted the comforts of her life and the freedom in her country, across the Atlantic in France citizens were still struggling for democracy.

The French had forever been ruled by monarchs and self-proclaimed emperors, and for too long the country had been experiencing wars and revolutions. Shortly after the United States had declared its independence from England in 1776 and established a democractic government, France plunged into the worst revolution of its history—one that lasted for ten years. The government was bankrupt, problems multiplied, and the dissatisfied people revolted against the aristocracy. King Louis XVI and Queen Marie Antoinette were put to death at the guillotine.

Soon afterward, Napoléon Bonaparte seized power in France and conquered much of Europe before he was defeated.

And now in 1865, France was under the despotic rule of

Bonaparte's nephew, Emperor Napoléon III, who lived in fear of being driven out of power by opposition fighting for a constitutional government. Constantly aware of the threat to his empire, he did everything he could to thwart his enemies. One incident involved the death of President Abraham Lincoln. After his assassination in Washington, many French citizens felt that they had lost a personal friend. They had admired him throughout his term of office, and that admiration deepened after he had freed the slaves. Now those people wanted to express their sympathy. Thousands began contributing money toward buying a gold medal, the size of a large coin, to present to Abraham Lincoln's widow.

Furious when he learned of this plan, Napoléon III tried to seize the money and list of contributors. It is not certain how much he disrupted the collection, but in the end he was unable to put a stop to it. Eventually the medal was made, and it was secretly arranged to be given to the American ambassador for presentation to Mrs. Lincoln. A young journalist took the ambassador aside during a meeting. "Tell Mrs. Lincoln," he said, "that in this little box is the heart of France." An accompanying letter explained that the commemorative medal was the gift of forty thousand citizens. Each had been asked to contribute no more than two cents in order to prove that this was truly an offering of the people.

The medal, now housed in the Library of Congress in Washington, D.C., was inscribed in French. The translation reads: "Dedicated by French democracy to Lincoln, twice-elected President of the United States—honest Lincoln who abolished slavery, reestablished the Union, and saved the Republic, without veiling the statue of liberty." The French did not literally mean a statue, but rather that Lincoln had saved the nation without dimming or clouding the image of liberty.

How strange and prophetic that the words *statue of liberty* were used before the thought of creating a real statue ever came to light.

It was only a short time afterward, though, that the idea was expressed more concretely. One night in a village near the palace of Versailles, outside of Paris, a man named Edouard René Lefebvre de Laboulaye gave a large dinner party in his home. Edouard, a politician, historian, and law professor, was a man who always praised America. His guests shared his feelings, and the dinner-table conversation centered around the topic of the United States, its politics, laws, and constitution, which assured liberty and equal rights to all of its citizens. Freedom, the men agreed, did not come easily.

Then Edouard, at the head of the table, spoke of the close connection between the two countries, which shared common thoughts and common struggles. After all, hadn't France supplied America with ships and weapons to help the people win their revolution? And hadn't George Washington made a lifelong friendship with the Marquis de Lafayette, the French statesman who became a major general in the American army during that war?

"There will always be a bond between the United States and France," said Edouard. "When two hearts have beaten together, something always remains, among nations as among individuals."

At that moment Edouard Laboulaye was struck with an idea. Why not build a monument that the French could give to America in the name of friendship! Why not build a monument that would show their own rulers how dedicated the people of France were to the ideal of liberty too!

Everyone listened attentively to Edouard's novel idea. There was one guest in particular, though, who thrilled at the sound of the word *monument*. He was the sculptor Frédéric Auguste Bartholdi, whom everyone called Auguste. How excited he was at the thought of building something so grand and passionate and stirring!

Frédéric Auguste Bartholdi, sculptor of the Statue of Liberty   LIBRARY OF CONGRESS

Furthermore, America would soon be celebrating its first century of independence, and if a statue could be presented in 1876, how especially meaningful it would be! Auguste's head was spinning with plans as he sat that night at his friend's dinner table.

4
The Language of Poetry

As Auguste was growing more and more excited at the thought of building the monument, Emma Lazarus was writing her first poems. She was discovering that, for her, poetry was a natural language.

It was only a short time before 1865, when she was fourteen, that she began to write. Dreamily she wrote of love found and lost, of aging and death, of the boundless joys of nature. Her mood was often melancholy, one of sweet sorrow, of bewitching sadness.

Even though her sister Josephine called Emma a born singer, she wrote later that Emma didn't "sing like a bird, from joy of being alive; and of being young, alas!" Josephine understood that Emma's unrelieved gloom was a "sign of youth, common especially among gifted persons whose sensibilities and imagination were not yet focused by reality."

In her ever-present sad and dreamy state, Emma wrote "The Echo."

When the shadows of evening fell low
    on the earth,
Then I climbed the steep side of the mount
    old and bare,
Whose dark, slender top seemed to cleave
    the blue air,
And then sadly I mused on the death
    of my love,
Looking down upon forest, and meadow,
    and grove.

Emma also liked to read the Greek and Roman classics, and she found that they were an important inspiration to her. When she wrote, she often imagined Aphrodite, the beautiful Olympian goddess of love, rising out of the sea on a cushion of foam; fair Apollo, god of music and light, riding in his swift chariot; and Daphne being changed into a laurel tree. There was something comforting in classic myths, which held that there was a unity between man and nature.

Still in her early teens, Emma began to immerse herself in the writings of the great essayist and philosopher, Ralph Waldo Emerson. He too had a passion for nature. Moved by his words, Emma wrote a short poem, "Links," in which she linked together heaven's brightness with some of the creatures of earth. Here she sang of how man's spirit and imagination could soar.

The little and the great are joined in one
By God's great force. The wondrous golden sun
Is linked unto the glow-worm's tiny spark;
The eagle soars to heaven in his flight;
And in those realms of space, all bathed in light,
Soar none except the eagle and the lark.

During the first few years that Emma was writing verse, the country was at war with itself. The ever-growing bitterness between the North and South over the issues of slavery and economy had finally reached a climax. On April 12,

1861, Confederate troops attacked Fort Sumter. No one knew how long the Civil War would last or how much bloodshed and grief would be left in its aftermath.

In the middle of the war, President Lincoln issued the Emancipation Proclamation, at last freeing the slaves in the United States. The movement to abolish the cruel system of slavery had seemed interminable to the abolitionists. How tragic it was that man had to be set against man to fight for the freedom that rightfully belonged to everyone.

It was not until April 9, 1865, that the South surrendered and the war finally came to an end. The country was exhausted and in deep pain from the loss of so many lives. There was hardly time for the country to catch its breath when only five days later the shocking event of President Abraham Lincoln's assassination at Ford's Theater took place.

Emma was fifteen then, far removed from the bloody battlefields, but she tried her hand at writing three poems on the theme of the Civil War. One was an elegy to a brigadier general who had died. Apparently she had read his name in the newspaper and chosen him as a symbolic representative of all soldiers who lost their lives.

Two other verses dealt with Lincoln's assassination, but not directly with Lincoln himself. Instead, Emma was thinking of the assassin, young John Wilkes Booth, injured in his escape from the theater. Emma wondered what he felt like being the object of a hunt and, pitying the fugitive, she wrote emotionally of what she imagined to be his "pain all the sleepless night."

Then, in the last poem, Emma turned her thoughts to Booth's mother and the woman's feelings for her son, who finally had been caught and killed and was now lying in "his flowerless grave."

Those lyric verses might not be the kind one would expect from such tragic and sweeping dramas, but Emma was distant from any worlds beyond her own safe one. Besides, whether experiencing it directly or from afar, war was hard to understand. Emma was learning to understand life from listening to the whispers of her own youthful heart.

During that same period, Emma's father retired from his business, even though he was only fifty-two. What would a man so devoted to his family do after retirement? He dismissed his children's tutors and took over the job himself. He hoped to further enrich his children's lives and education, exposing them to new areas of literature, history, and music. The girls, and especially Emma, became more attached than ever to him. Although young ladies of class were always protected by their fathers then, in the Lazarus household it seemed to be to the extreme. Emma rarely left the family and made little effort to make friends her age.

She was much too content at home. Reading and writing filled her hours. Within two years she had collected a sheaf of thirty-five poems, including a sixty-page blank verse narrative she entitled "Bertha." It was a melodramatic story, full of romance, gothic mystery, tragedy, and evil. Placed in an eleventh-century castle in France, it begins with an innocent wedding between the beautiful Bertha and her beloved Robert. But from the start their love is foreshadowed with doom. Shortly after the vows are exchanged, it is learned that the bride and groom are first cousins and that such a marriage is forbidden. Swooning into a coma, Bertha gives birth to a prince. She awakens in a monastery, where a cruel abbot has drowned her child and substituted a deformed foundling. At the end, Bertha falls at the altar and is declared by the priests to be dead. It is a spiritual death about which the poet speaks.

Emma had a first cousin believed to be the object of her affection, and she dedicated one of her poems to him. But it seems he did not care for her in return. The cousin, Washington Nathan, the son of her mother's brother, was a handsome young man who won favors from a number of girls who crossed his path.

No longer only imagining the joys and sorrows of love, Emma for the first time tasted a bit of life, although it never developed into a full experience. Emotionally distraught, the teenage girl wrote of "desires and yearnings that may find no rest," a "craving sense of emptiness and pain," and "grief to be conquered day by day."

All of these feelings, though, were hidden from her family. In her solitude it was only with her pen that she expressed her emotions.

During the time when Emma had such a steady outpouring of poems, she also began to translate works from two European poets, the Frenchman Victor Hugo and the German Heinrich Heine. Hugo was a romantic and melancholy writer, to whom Emma felt drawn. Heine had a love for beauty and the classics. He was a Jew who only a few years before his death came to feel a sentiment toward his Jewish heritage. Could it have been that Emma, while reading and translating his poetry, was beginning to stir with feelings toward her heritage of Judaism too?

Her ever-devoted father brought together the translations and her thirty-five original poems to have them bound. Few women had their works published during those years. Some were bold enough to submit their manuscripts under men's names. In France, Amantine Aurore Lucile Dupin took the pen name George Sand. English novelist Mary Ann (later Marian) Evans chose George Eliot. Even the Brontë sisters, who eventually did publish under their own names, submitted their first work under the guise of male authorship.

But Emma's father decided it would be all right to have his daughter's poems printed for the family and friends. Under the circumstances, he concluded, a small private volume could certainly bear her own name. So he took the poems to the publisher H. O. Houghton and Company and arranged for the printing. The title of the book was *Poems and Translations by Emma Lazarus, written between the ages of Fourteen and Sixteen*. The poet dedicated it to her father.

Emma was very proud of her efforts. So was her family. Soon someone else, an extremely well known and brilliant writer of the nineteenth century, would meet her and ask that she send him a copy of her newly published book.

5
The Sculptor Sees America

In the spring of 1871, Auguste Bartholdi set sail from Paris on the S.S. *Pereire*. It was six years since the night of his friend's dinner party, and talk of building a statue for America had never ceased. Now Auguste was on his way to see the land of democracy for himself. He wanted to meet the people and get a feeling for the national character.

The sea was stormy at first, the ship rocking and creaking, but no matter to Auguste. He still called himself the most excited passenger on board. He was on a mission, one that would take vision, and perhaps even genius.

Of course, he realized that the first job that lay ahead of him was selling the idea to America. But how could he expect to do that? After all, he didn't even have as much as a rough sketch of a liberty statue.

Then, as the winds eased and the sea calmed, the sculptor took to sitting outdoors on a deck chair with a sketch pad in his lap. He gazed out over the vast expanse of ocean, wondering how to portray the concept of freedom. What did freedom look like? He had studied the American silver dollar, which bore the portrait of a woman's head in profile. He had asked himself if there were a famous man who would embody the idea, but he found no answer to that question. He had wandered through museums and looked through books of reproduced paintings. It was indeed baffling.

Then one calm and peaceful evening Auguste thought of something Edouard Laboulaye had said. "Liberty is the mother of a family that watches over the cradle of her children, that protects consciences. . . . Liberty is the sister of Justice and of Mercy, mother of Equality, Abundance, and Peace."

That was it! His idea was born. His monument would be a proud, tall woman, and she would have one arm raised, holding a torch.

Now he began to make sketch after sketch. Having an idea didn't mean he could translate it perfectly to paper right away, though. The first several drawings were unsatisfactory to him. One by one he tossed them overboard, watching them flutter in the wind and fall gently to the ocean below.

Later sketches pleased him more, so he began putting them away in his cabin. It was especially hard to know what kind of pedestal would be erected. His drawings showed one that was considerably smaller than the pedestal that came to be. But the early drawings he saved were those of a woman with a torch and a crown of rays upon her head.

The idea of a robed woman was not a completely new one. In ancient Roman times, a temple had been built to a robed goddess in the third century B.C. The female figure then signified religious or political virtues.

In early June the steamer approached New York Harbor, and suddenly a tiny island came into view. To Auguste it seemed to be the gateway to America. "Yes, in this very place shall be raised the Statue of Liberty," he wrote home, "as grand as the idea which it embodies, casting radiance upon the two worlds." The sculptor sketched the island too.

The most excited passenger on board was not disappointed at his arrival. He described the moment: "When after some days of voyaging—in the pearly radiance of a beautiful morning is revealed the magnificent spectacle of those immense cities, of those rivers extending as far as the eye can reach, festooned with masts and flags . . . it is thrilling. It is indeed the New World which appears in its majestic expanse with the ardor of its glowing life. . . ."

Auguste's trip did not include a view of Castle Garden, once a fortress, then a concert hall, and finally a station through which newly arrived refugees passed. After all, Auguste had not journeyed on an immigrant ship, so he had no opportunity to pass through it.

During the year of his visit, two hundred fifty thousand refugees from all corners of the world went through the portals of Castle Garden in lower New York, although they did not all settle in the city. But wherever they went, their communities benefited from the new skills they brought with them and from their eagerness to work. They were helping to build America.

In New York, Auguste did not see the slums where the immigrants lived and worked; or the crowded, unsanitary tenement conditions; or the factory sweatshops where young and old toiled twelve hours a day in dimly lit and poorly ventilated rooms. Beyond New York, he did not see the poor mining towns of Pennsylvania or the mills of Massachusetts. He did not see the courageous immigrants who built the railways or the pioneers who ventured west.

When Auguste Bartholdi dreamed of and planned his monument, he gave almost no thought to the immigrants at all. How was he, or anyone for that matter, to know what the statue would come to mean to millions of refugees yet to set out for America?

Certainly the new country offered opportunities, but not everyone could become a millionaire like the fur trader and

Upon landing in America, immigrants passed through Castle Garden in lower Manhattan.   NATIONAL PARK SERVICE: STATUE OF LIBERTY NATIONAL MONUMENT

real-estate genius John Jacob Astor. Most couldn't even approach making a fortune, although more and more, new Americans were shaping comfortable lives for themselves. The fact was, though, that poverty was everywhere. Horace Greeley, editor of the New York *Tribune* and a reform-minded man, often reported on the gap between the wealthy and the victims of poverty. Once he wrote of a brilliant and fashionably dressed crowd attending the Astor Place Opera House while elsewhere on the same night "in dark and dreary alleys, barefooted and ragged children delve among filth for bones and cinders."

The former slaves, freed less than a decade earlier, remained poor and struggling. They had no education and few skills. They were given no land and little help from the government. What more could be expected of them?

The darker and more desolate side of American life that

Auguste missed was a world also unfamiliar to Emma Lazarus. But unlike Emma, Auguste managed to see more of
the country in six months than young Emma had seen in
her whole life.

Perhaps as Auguste strolled the finer neighborhoods of
New York that summer, he passed Emma's house. The
sculptor and the poet were never actually to meet. But if he
did chance to turn off Fifth Avenue and strut along West
Fourteenth Street, that could have been the one brief moment they might have crossed paths. Only the fruits of their
artistic efforts would join them someday, when Emma's
words would add so much meaning to Auguste's brilliant
monument.

Whom did Auguste meet, then, and what did he see on
his historic visit? He arrived with letters of introduction to
wealthy and important people. He met influential men and
women, whom he, Edouard, and the French statue committee hoped would be able to help France in its quest for
democracy. He even spent some time with President Ulysses S. Grant in his summer home in Long Branch, New Jer-
sey, where the two men smoked cigars together in the garden. Auguste met a number of other politicians, and several
men who had been active abolitionists. He spoke with the
artist John La Farge, poet Henry Wadsworth Longfellow,
newspaper editor Horace Greeley, and an architect by the
name of Richard Morris Hunt.

Wherever Auguste went, he was cordially received, and
so was his idea for the statue. He was not able to speak English perfectly, but he was charming and presented the idea
with lively enthusiasm. With many of his new acquain-
tances, he shared feelings about the anxiety of exile and the
struggle for freedom. At the time he made his ocean voyage, he knew these troubles personally. Only recently France
had been defeated by Prussia in the Franco-Prussian War,
and his town in the province of Alsace, including his own
mother's home, had been occupied for a time by enemy

troops. Most of Alsace was not returned to France until after World War I, several decades later.

While still in New York, he sent Edouard a sincere and honest letter of his impressions. "I am still somewhat too new here to dare express myself," he wrote. "The view of New York has rather startled me; I feel a great admiration for the institutions of the country, for the patriotism and sense of duty of the citizens, for the impersonality of the administration. Yet my old European shell is a bit chilled by the ruling material sense of affairs. Their way of life seems to leave the Americans without time to live. Their habits and conventions are not in accord with my idea. Everything here is big, even the *petits pois* [peas]."

Auguste left the New York area to "see a most varied world." He traveled from east to west, then north to south. He passed through the Ohio and Mississippi valleys, saw prairie dogs and buffalos, Indian villages and small towns, and in California he toured picturesque Spanish missions.

"In every town I look for people who may wish to take part in our enterprise," he wrote Edouard toward the end of his travels. "So far I have found them everywhere; the ground is well prepared; only the spark will have to be provided by a manifestation on the part of France."

6

An Artist Struggles

One winter evening in New York, Mr. and Mrs. Lazarus attended a party at the home of a friend, the prominent banker Samuel Gray Ward, and Emma was invited to come along.

When they arrived, Emma's father led her toward a gentleman seated in the parlor. She had never seen him before, but he looked grand and distinguished. Suddenly Emma found herself being introduced to him.

Who was this elderly gentleman? He was none other than Ralph Waldo Emerson, the essayist, lecturer, and great thinker of the day. And he was Emma's idol. Emma was nearly struck speechless!

Mr. Emerson was visiting from his home in Concord, Massachusetts, a city known for its circle of writers who were bringing new ideas and literature to America. Without question, he was one of its leading figures. His poetry and writings on nature as a gateway to true experience were a beacon to Emma. His essays on self-reliance and his impressions of everyday life were an inspiration. Josephine said that for her younger sister, Mr. Emerson's works had become "bread and wine."

At last Emma was able to gain enough composure to speak to him. She told him how much she admired his work and that she read some of it over and over. Then, her head bowed slightly and her voice lowered, Emma said that she wrote poetry and that she even had a book published.

Mr. Emerson smiled. Would she be able to send a copy of that book to him? he asked. Emma could hardly believe what he was saying. Wasn't it exciting enough to meet the great man? But to have him ask to read her poetry! That was more than anything she dared to dream.

It did not take long for her to send the book, which she inscribed and dated February 12, 1868. Thus began a correspondence that was to last for several years.

"I have so happy recollections of the conversation at Mr. Ward's," Mr. Emerson wrote after receiving the package, "that I am glad to have them confirmed by the possession of your book and letter. The poems have important merits." Of "Bertha," the story about the doomed marriage, he said he found it awfully "tragic and painful" and warned her against beginning a story on such a sad note.

But how thrilled Emma was that he responded, and how encouraged that he said he was glad to have her book.

During their exchange of letters, Emma thanked him again and again for his attention and for allowing her the privilege of writing to him. Her humility sometimes caused her to write that she feared she was sending him "unworthy verses."

Mr. Emerson's letters often sounded like those of a stern teacher. He offered praise where he thought it was due, but he never hesitated to give constructive criticism when he found reason. More than once he recommended that Emma read Shakespeare as a model of language economy. He thought she used too many words to express a thought or

The renowned writer Ralph Waldo Emerson played an
important role in encouraging Emma's literary career.
LIBRARY OF CONGRESS

image when fewer and more precise ones would do better.
Sometimes he made other reading suggestions, such as
Henry David Thoreau and Walt Whitman, whose works, like
Mr. Emerson's, were also in harmony with nature.

Before long, though, Mr. Emerson, the master and teacher,
began to realize that Emma spent too much time reading and
not enough time experiencing life. "Books are a safe ground,
and a long one," he wrote, "but still introductory only, for
what we really seek is ever comparison of experiences—to
know if you have found therein what I prize, or still better
if you have found what I have never found, and yet is admirable to me also."

Despite his direct criticism, Emma treasured his friendship and guidance. He had advised many eager young people who sought his wisdom and yearned for inspiration, and Emma came to write of him: "To how many thousand youthful hearts has not his word been the beacon—nay, more, the guiding star—that led them safely through periods of mental storm and struggle."

Certainly he spurred her on—to strive, to reach higher and for the more noble in her work—and she did begin to grow as a poet. The mastery of her craft improved, and she was now, lamp in hand, searching deeper into the soul. Although she was still overly dramatic and sentimental, some of the dark and heavy clouds that loomed over her slowly began to lift, and like Emerson, she took comfort in nature. She wrote that it was good to be alive, "to see the light that plays upon the grass, to feel the mild breezes stir . . . to gaze at the bright, breathing sea."

A new maturity was seen in a poem called "Heroes." Emma thought of the aftermath of the Civil War, not only about the tears shed for the brave dead but also about the feelings for the ones who went on living.

> They who were brave to act,
> And rich enough their action to forget;
> Who, having filled their day with chivalry,
> Withdraw and keep their simpleness intact,
> And all unconscious add more lustre yet
> Unto their victory.

She wrote further of the farmers and the city dwellers, and then she went on to write sympathetically of the scarred veterans.

> Maimed, helpless, lingering still
> through suffering years,
> May they not envy now the restful sleep
> Of the dear fellow-martyrs they survive?

For Emma, all those who went on living and working from day to day had become the real heroes of the nation.

When Emma turned twenty-one, a second book was published, this time without her father's help and for a wider audience. It was called *Admetus and Other Poems*. Before its printing, she had sent the title work to Mr. Emerson, who wrote a letter full of admiration.

> My dear friend,
>
> I write immediately on closing my first entire reading of "Admetus," to say, All Hail! You have written a noble poem, which I cannot enough praise. You have hid yourself from me until now, for the merits of the preceding poems did not unfold this fulness & high equality of power. . . . I think I shall return the treasured sheets by tomorrow's mail, secure that the eternal Apollo & the placated Fates will guard them to you.
>
> R. W. Emerson

Was it any wonder that Emma was ecstatic to receive such a complimentary letter! "Admetus" had not been easy to write. A great deal of work had gone into retelling the story of the ancient Greek legend in blank verse. Admetus was the king of Thessaly, who lived happily with his lovely queen, Alcestis. Admetus, though, was afraid of dying early, and when it came to pass that he must die, he set about searching for someone to die in his stead. His queen loved him so dearly she gladly agreed to give her life for his, and he allowed it. After her death, grief in the palace was so unbearable that the gods finally returned Alcestis to life.

Emma dedicated the poem "to my friend Ralph Waldo Emerson."

It was wonderful to be admired and published, but growing as an artist did not mean meeting only with success. Mr. Emerson submitted the poem to his friend William Dean Howells, editor of the popular magazine, the *Atlantic Monthly*, but he turned it down. As soon as Mr. Emerson heard the

Engraving of Emma Lazarus   NATIONAL PARK SERVICE:
STATUE OF LIBERTY NATIONAL MONUMENT

news, he wrote and assured Emma that if it had been his magazine, he would have printed it "thankfully and proudly." He also pointed out something important for her to understand as an artist. Literary tastes were subject to whim, he said. What one critic disliked, another could find to be of high merit. But still, the rejection hurt, and Emma had to learn to accept it if she were going to believe in herself as a poet.

Happily "Admetus" eventually appeared in another publication, *Lippincott's Magazine*, which during the next few years was to print many of her poems. In addition, "Admetus" was well received in literary groups far from New York and Concord—across the Atlantic in England. *Scribner's Monthly* magazine began to print Emma's work also, and her readership began to grow.

In Emma's new book there appeared a poem that was to become especially important in her development as an artist. It was her first verse dealing with a Jewish theme.

One summer during the family's stay in Newport, they visited the synagogue there. It was a building dedicated in colonial days, in 1763, and Emma found its history fascinating. After New Amsterdam, the colony of Rhode Island opened its doors to Jews in 1658. Its founder, Roger Williams, stood staunchly for religious freedom. The Jews were few in number and had no place of their own to worship, so they took turns holding services in their private homes. A century later, there was a large enough congregation to erect a building, and they appealed for funds to construct a synagogue, which they came to call Yeshuat Israel, "salvation of Israel." The first contribution came from none other than Shearith Israel in New York.

Not long after the synagogue's completion, the city of Newport was honored by a visit from the country's most famous patriot—George Washington. In a letter, the synagogue congregation welcomed and praised him, and in response, President Washington sent a letter, dated August 17, 1790, "To the Hebrew Congregation in Newport, R.I." It was a declaration of religious liberty in the United States. Jeshuat Israel, as it is known today, more often called Touro Synagogue, remains at the same location on Touro Street in Newport, and George Washington's letter is on display for the congregation and for visitors. In 1946, the synagogue was designated a national historical site.

At the time of Emma's visit, though, it was temporarily inactive and several years away from being restored and opened once again. Emma walked about the dusty, decaying building. She was quiet and pensive as she looked at the beautiful landmark. There was the ark with its Torahs, the sacred teachings, which were covered with Sephardic-style mantles. There were five brass chandeliers, Greek-style Corinthian and Ionic columns, and a painting of the Ten Commandments. There was even an old matzo board, the

Touro Synagogue in Newport, Rhode Island, the subject of
Emma's poem "In the Jewish Synagogue at Newport"
COURTESY OF THE SOCIETY OF FRIENDS OF TOURO SYNAGOGUE

size of a small tabletop, which had been used to prepare the
matzo dough for Passover.

Then, carefully, Emma stepped up onto the *bimah*, where
the cantors had stood to lead the congregations. But she
discovered something strange and intriguing. It looked like
a trap door on the floor of the *bimah*. Slowly Emma bent
down, opened it, and found herself staring into a deep and
secret-looking tunnel. Whatever was it doing there?

Emma learned that, like her father's ancestors, the first
Jews of Newport had come from Spain and Portugal. They
remembered how the Marranos had to practice their Judaism in hiding. Of course, in America no one had to hide,
but the congregation decided to build the tunnel as a symbolic reminder to their children so they would be aware of
the difficult times of the past and would value their freedom in the new land.

Emma was moved by what she saw and heard. It started her thinking about Hebrew civilizations and the significance of death beyond her own imagined personal loss, and she sat down to write "In the Jewish Synagogue at Newport," which was printed in the *Jewish Messenger*.

Here, where the noises of the busy town,
    The ocean's plunge and roar can enter not,
We stand and gaze around with tearful awe,
    And muse upon the consecrated spot.

No signs of life are here: the very prayers
    Inscribed around are in a language dead;
The light of the "perpetual lamp" is spent
    That an undying radiance was to shed.

What prayers were in this temple offered up,
    Wrung from sad hearts that knew no joy on earth,
By these lone exiles of a thousand years,
    From the fair sunrise land that gave them birth!

She goes on to speak of the perpetual lamp, a light that remains forever lit above the ark holding the sacred Torahs in every synagogue. And further on in the poem, she writes of "this new world of light." Such words were to be used by Emma in many of her poems as symbols of lighting the way toward truth.

After the publication of Emma's second book, she decided to try writing something other than lyrical, dramatic, or narrative verse. This time she wrote a novel, which she called *Alide*. It was not an original story, though, but one based on the life of the German poet Goethe.

During the year of *Alide*'s publication, 1874, two other important events occurred that deeply affected Emma's life. They were both unhappy, and both caused Emma wounds that would take time to heal.

In April her mother died. For the first time, the close Lazarus family was broken apart. How painful it was for Emma, but at least she and her father and sisters and brother had one another for solace and comfort. Emma, of course, also had another way to express her pain, and so she sat down and wrote a number of poems dealing with her most private feelings and thoughts.

The other event involved Mr. Emerson. For some years, he had been collecting poetry that especially pleased him. And now the poems had been published in a book he called *Parnassus*. With her heart pounding, Emma bought a copy of the new anthology, opened it, and began to leaf through the pages. It looked as if there were more than one hundred and fifty poets represented. And maybe thirty or forty of them were American. Emma turned page after page, looking, hoping, but she could not deny the terrible truth. She was not included. Not even one small verse. And after all his kind attention and all his encouraging words! Emma was devastated.

Mr. Emerson had told her of the whims of literary taste, but she had never imagined that there wasn't one of her verses he didn't like well enough to include in such a large collection. What a truly painful experience!

Engulfed with despair, Emma decided to write to him:

> I cannot resist the impulse of expressing to you my extreme disappointment at finding you have so far modified the enthusiastic estimate you held of my literary labors as to refuse me a place in the large & miscellaneous collection of poems you have just published. I can only consider this omission a public retraction of all the flattering opinions & letters you have sent me. . . .

Had she done anything to forfeit his friendship? she asked. And what was she to think now? Did he change his mind about the compliments he paid her, or did he not intend to pay them at all? In ending her letter, she asked him to respond at his earliest convenience.

Emma mailed the letter. No matter what his reply, Emma was certain she could no longer continue to be his friend.

7
"My Daughter, Liberty"

When Auguste returned to Paris, he could hardly wait to begin work on the statue. He was, after all, an artist, a sculptor, a man of vision, and creative work was what he liked doing best.

But how could he proceed with such an immense undertaking without first facing and overcoming the obstacles in his way?

Fortunately there was no government opposition, as there had been when President Lincoln's widow was given the gold medal several years earlier. The political climate had changed. The French had revolted against Napoléon III, and with his deposition, the tradition of despotic rulers ended. At long last, a constitutional government had been formed, but welcomed as it was, citizens still found it short of the goals they wanted. They continued to work toward stronger leadership and for a more stable government.

Auguste was faced with finding a studio more spacious than his own and hiring enough good workmen for the task that lay ahead. He also had decisions to make about materials to use for such a colossal statue. But those matters would have to wait until he solved the most pressing problem of all—the financial one. Where would the money come from? Auguste had little taste for business affairs, but he had no choice other than to begin attending public functions and giving speeches to solicit funds.

The first and most important event took place at the Hôtel du Louvre in Paris. In a room decorated with red, white, and blue, some two hundred men, both American and French, gathered, and a committee headed by Edouard Laboulaye was formed. After the meal the guests listened to Auguste describe his plans for the statue. The measurements sounded impressive enough, but when Auguste told them that people would actually be able to climb up inside the statue, the guests were astonished. French francs worth thousands of dollars were pledged that night. Unfortunately, though, dinners that followed were not as successful, and funding was to become a constant worry.

Meanwhile, there was at least enough money for Auguste to begin work. During the weeks he was searching for a studio, he started shaping small clay models. He saw how he needed to form the statue with one foot forward for balance. Auguste also gave much thought to the statue's face. He wanted it to show suffering, yet reveal strength. Whom could he use for a model? The perfect person, he decided, was his beloved mother. Some people thought Charlotte Bartholdi looked too grim and severe, but not Auguste. To him, his mother's face embodied all the characteristics he wished to portray.

In her personal relationship to her son, it was believed she controlled him too much. Auguste had fallen in love with a woman named Jeanne-Emilie Baheux de Puysieux, but his mother disapproved of her because she was only a seamstress. Auguste couldn't bring himself to ask for Jeanne-Emilie's hand in marriage, knowing it would upset his mother.

At last Auguste found a spacious studio to rent. It was in a workshop owned by Gaget, Gauthier and Co. With his plans and blueprints spread out in front of him, he explained to the craftsmen his approach to building the one hundred fifty-one-foot-high project. How amazed the craftsmen were! And what an extraordinary architectural and engineering task they had ahead of them!

Of course, Auguste needed more than carpenters and sculptors. It was also necessary to have someone build a frame to which the exterior metal could be fastened. One man offered to build one of steel. He was Alexandre Gustave Eiffel, who became famous years later as the builder of the Eiffel Tower in Paris. At the time, though, he made steel bridges. Alexandre Eiffel welcomed the new challenge.

Men at work on the arm and hand of the Statue of Liberty in the Paris studio of Gaget, Gauthier and Co.   RARE BOOK DIVISION, THE NEW YORK PUBLIC LIBRARY; ASTOR, LENOX AND TILDEN FOUNDATIONS

Construction of the Statue of Liberty progresses, on a steel
frame built by Alexandre Gustave Eiffel.

With the problem of the frame solved, Auguste faced another decision. What material would he use to form the statue? Stone was too heavy. Bronze was also heavy and expensive as well. His choice was copper. It was light and, above all, durable. First the statue sections would be made in plaster. Then wooden molds would be cast and, after that, thin sheets of copper hammered into the wooden molds. That way the copper sheets would come out as exact replicas of the plaster model.

Continually plagued with financial troubles, Auguste alternately started and stopped work. Eleven years had passed since the monument had first been discussed. By 1876, the year of America's centennial celebration—the time when France had hoped to present its gift—Liberty Enlightening the World was still a long way from completion. The best Auguste could do to join the celebration was to send part of the statue for the International Exhibition in Philadelphia. He chose the arm and the torch it held.

Scores of men toiled from dawn until dusk to complete the forty-two-foot arm. Then the parts were packed, taking twenty-one crates to hold them. As the official French representative to the exhibit, Auguste left once more for the United States. This time he saw Castle Garden, the depot building through which immigrants were passing every day. Along with other statue committee members and several land surveyors, he took a boat out to look over Bedloe's Island in detail. Nonchalantly Auguste remarked that he thought it would be nice if the name could be changed to Liberty Island. He did not mention it again on that trip, but it was not completely forgotten.

When Auguste arrived in Philadelphia for the exhibit, he found the heat unbearable. That summer it was recorded that twenty-one trolley horses dropped dead on Market Street. But the weather was not the only problem for Auguste. In New York and Philadelphia he found no enthusiasm for the

The right arm and torch of the statue are displayed in Philadelphia during America's centennial celebration, at the International Exhibition in 1876.   MUSEUM OF THE CITY OF NEW YORK

statue he had been laboring on year after year. How grim he felt. But he refused to let his spirits be dampened for long. "My courage will never fail," he wrote Edouard. Auguste realized that he had been wrong in going only to the wealthy for support. It was clear now that he needed to solicit public support.

While in the United States, he became courageous in love too. He sent for Jeanne-Emilie and married her in the home of his friend, artist John La Farge, who lived in Newport.

There is no chance that Auguste met Emma Lazarus in Newport at the time. The small, private wedding was held in December, when the Lazarus beach house was locked for the winter.

When Auguste returned to Paris with his bride, happily she and his mother became friends despite Charlotte Bartholdi's feelings that Jeanne-Emilie came from a lower social class. Auguste settled into married life and returned to the studio, where the woman with the torch continued to grow. Auguste began calling her "my daughter, Liberty." She was out in the courtyard now, rising up among the scaffolding and above a sea of Parisian houses. French people and foreign tourists alike stopped and gazed in awe. A New York *World* reporter described a scene of several workmen scampering back and forth, hammering here and there, all on one bit of the statue's hair.

In 1878, Miss Liberty's gleaming copper head went on a carriage ride to a prominent display spot at the Paris World's Fair. Former U.S. president Ulysses S. Grant visited Paris that year and was astonished at what he saw. It was simply amazing, he said, to look at eyes that each measured two-and-a-half feet in length!

That year Auguste received good news. At last America was doing its part. A committee had been appointed, and headed by the then secretary of state, William M. Evarts, and as agreed, the committee would see to it that funds were collected. Auguste's daughter, Liberty, would have a pedestal after all.

8
What Kind of Poet Am I?

Mr. Emerson never replied to the anguished letter that Emma wrote. What a mixture of sadness and bitterness she felt, and how long she carried the burden inside her! Gradually she even began to experience feelings of serious self-doubt. Was her work really of any merit?

When all was considered, though, Emma knew she could never give up writing. Poetry for her was like breathing. It was her life.

Then, one day in 1876 an envelope addressed to Emma arrived. It was from Mr. Emerson. And after not hearing a word from him for two years! Emma tore open the envelope and found not a letter but a wonderful surprise—an invitation from him and Mrs. Emerson to spend a week at their home.

Was there ever any question that her unhappiness about being left out of Mr. Emerson's anthology, *Parnassus*, would cause her to turn down his invitation? Certainly not. By then Emma had matured and come to understand more about herself. To refuse such an invitation would be foolish. She never was to learn the reason for being excluded from the anthology. The subject was not discussed with Mr. Emerson at all.

In August, Emma boarded a train in New York for Concord. She was twenty-seven years old, and it was her first trip without her family. How excited she was! Once she had been thrilled to receive a short letter from Mr. Emerson. Now she was going to be a guest in his home!

Emerson was nearly seventy-five years old at the time Emma came to visit. Along with his wife and daughter Ellen, he met Emma at the train station with his one-horse wagon. On the way to his home, Emma had her first sights of Concord, "lovely and smiling, with its quiet meadows, quiet slopes, and quietest of rivers." Not only was Emma a soaring spirit now. She was also the lark she had once written about, stretching her wings, taking flight, singing, observing, questioning.

The week was filled with awe and wonder, and Concord was full of interesting and gracious men and women. The novelist Nathaniel Hawthorne was a neighbor and so was the Alcott family. The second oldest Alcott daughter, Louisa May, had authored a number of children's books, including *Little Women*, which had been very popular since its publication in two volumes seven and eight years earlier. Her father, Amos Bronson Alcott, was a critic and social reformer, and had been an abolitionist.

She also met William Ellery Channing, a poet and the biographer of Henry David Thoreau, who several years earlier had tragically died of tuberculosis just before his forty-fifth birthday. Thoreau, long devoted to Emerson, was hailed as a brilliant man. He had become most well known for an experiment in simple living.

On a small parcel of land on Emerson's property, near Walden Pond, Thoreau had built a one-room cabin, and furnished it with a bed, table, and chair, all of which he had made himself. He grew his own vegetables, cut firewood, swam in the pond, took long walks, and lived in communion with the animals and birds. Much of his time in solitude was spent reading and writing. He wrote *Walden*, a celebration of the harmony between man and nature. He urged man to "live deeply and suck out all the marrow of life."

Thoreau also attacked social institutions like slavery, which he believed was immoral. He wrote a social protest essay, "Civil Disobedience," in which he said that the government must recognize the individual as a higher and more independent power and treat him accordingly. The essay came to influence many reformers, including Mahatma Gandhi and Martin Luther King, Jr.

Now Mr. Channing guided Emma out to Walden Pond. "He took me through the the woods," she wrote, "and pointed out to me every spot visited and described by his friend. Where the hut stood is a little pile of stones, and a sign, 'Site of Thoreau's Hut,' and a few steps beyond is the pond with thickly-wooded shores—everything exquisitely peaceful and beautiful in the afternoon light. . . ."

Emma realized that Mr. Channing did not usually warm up to strangers. But she understood why he took a liking to her. "The bond of our sympathy," she wrote, "was my admiration for Thoreau, whose memory he actually worships, having been his companion in his best days, and his daily attendant in the last years of illness and heroic suffering. I do not know whether I was most touched by the thought of the unique, lofty character that had inspired this depth and fervor of friendship, or by the pathetic constancy and pure affection of the poor, desolate old man before me, who tried to conceal his tenderness and sense of irremediable loss by a show of gruffness."

When they parted, Mr. Channing gave Emma a gift. It was not just any gift, but his own book on Thoreau and the pocket compass Thoreau had used when he took his walks. Emma was filled with gratitude at receiving such treasured keep-sakes.

While in Concord, Emma showed Mr. Emerson proof sheets of a verse drama she called *The Spagnoletto* [The Little Spaniard], which she had brought along. It was a tragedy set in Italy in 1655. In it a painter so deeply loves his daughter that he keeps her locked up. At last the inexperienced girl runs away with a duke who eventually betrays her. The father, distraught and humiliated, can no longer paint. Furious with shame, he disguises himself as a monk and follows his daughter. Then he commits suicide in her presence.

It's not difficult to see the parallels between the girl in the drama and Emma's own life. Emma and her father were uncommonly devoted to each other, and that was more than likely one of the reasons Emma was not comfortable meeting men her own age. She was never to love another man or to marry. One writer, H. E. Jacob, has written that *The Spagnoletto* was a "choked outcry of the writer herself."

Whatever the psychological implications of the drama, as a work of art it failed. It was criticized for lacking heroic action and, worse, for lacking a character with whom the reader or audience could truly sympathize or care about.

Emma wrote later to her new Concord friend, Ellen, "I have given up all dreams of having my play produced on the stage—I am afraid it is not actable."

Although Emma showed the proof sheets to Mr. Emerson before she left Concord, he was unable to give them his full attention. Advancing in age, he was beginning to have memory lapses. Emma was not disheartened this time, though. She understood a great deal more than she had in the past. And while she had appreciated his criticism and continued to respect him, she realized that she was no longer completely under his spell. His opinion was not the only one that mattered. His ideas were not the only ideas that were important. The visit had been lovely, and she would not have missed it for anything in the world.

When Emma returned home, her family began preparing a move uptown to 34 East Fifty-seventh Street, another wealthy area in the city. To Emma, it became a time to reflect on the home where she had grown up. It also became a time during which she began to wonder about her life, brood about her purpose.

What kind of poet am I? she began to ask herself. For whom do I speak? The more she reflected on these questions, the more uncertain she felt about her identity.

She wanted to belong to womanhood, to the literary world, to all of humanity. She wanted to hold an important place. But she didn't feel a sense of fitting in anywhere. Her poems seemed small and trivial, perhaps too personal. The classical themes she used weren't popular anymore, and there was an increasing awareness for her that the worship of beauty, art for art's sake, could sometimes be empty. Her lamplight seemed to be dimming, and she was losing her way.

Literary friends listened sympathetically and offered kind advice. Edmund Clarence Stedman, a banker, poet and critic, was a friend she could speak to openly and directly. In a particularly gloomy mood one day, Emma said to him, "I have accomplished nothing to stir, nothing to awaken, to teach or to suggest, nothing that the world could not equally do without."

Mr. Stedman listened patiently and then he quietly suggested that she think of the heritage of the Jewish people. Could that not be a wonderful inspiration? he asked. Was there not a wealth in this subject for a poet of her sensitivity and mind?

No, she did not consider herself a Jewish writer, Emma answered. She was proud of her religion and ancestry, she insisted, but she felt more an American than a Jew.

Mr. Stedman argued no further. He knew that it would be of no avail to tell a poet what to write about. Ultimately it was Emma's choice.

But something was stirring inside Emma already, even if she wasn't consciously aware of it. She had written about the Touro Synagogue, and she had continued to translate the poetry of Heinrich Heine, but now she was translating works of three medieval Hebrew poets—Solomon Ben Judah Gabirol, Judah Ben Ha-Levi, and Moses Ben Esra—and the *Jewish Messenger* was printing them. Of course, she wasn't versed in the Hebrew language, so her method was to translate into English from the German versions that most appealed to her.

Slowly Emma was moving in a new direction, but she was still unsure of herself and proceeded gingerly. One day a new acquaintance, Dr. Gustav Gottheil, the rabbi of Temple Emanu-El, asked her if she would translate some hymns and write a few original ones for a hymnal he was preparing to publish.

Emma was glad to set to work on the translations, but she would write no original hymns. "The flesh is willing," she wrote to Dr. Gottheil, explaining her reason, "but the spirit is weak. I should be most happy to serve you in your difficult and patriotic undertaking, but the more I see of these religious poems, the more I feel that the fervor and enthusiasm . . . are altogether lacking in me." She was not ready to commit herself to writing her own verse with a Jewish theme.

Not long afterward, though, Emma found herself reading a detailed narrative account about a tragic historical event that so absorbed her, she could not get it out of her mind.

It was about an epidemic disease that in the fourteenth century swept across China, India, Persia, and finally Europe. In Europe it destroyed nearly a third of the population. It was called bubonic plague and became known as the Black Death. This wretched disease was transmitted to human beings by fleas from infected rats. No one escaped suffering, no man, woman, or child, whether Christian, Jew, Islamic, or Mongol. Everyone was devastated with equal terror and with equal pain.

In those days, the plague's cause was a mystery. There

was no scientific explanation. And when a disaster of such proportions is unexplainable, people sometimes invent their own reasons. This time the Christians turned toward the Jews in accusation. The Jews caused the Black Death, they cried, by poisoning the wells.

It did not occur to them that the Jews were drinking the water too. They had their answer, and the rumor spread so quickly, there was no stopping it. So in city after city, the Jews were set upon and beaten to death or burned at the stake.

The narrative haunted Emma. In the past when she read of other events in history, they had held mostly a literary interest for her. But this was different. This struck her as being deeply significant because it spoke of mankind everywhere, throughout all ages. It was an event that concerned human suffering, man's cruelty to man, injustice, and religious persecution. It also brought up the issue of truth in human relationships.

These were the kinds of themes that would be truly meaningful to write about, Emma realized. No poem dealing with them would be trivial. She need not have a small voice. She was sincerely moved now to try a new voice, one that had something important to say.

Perhaps she was thinking of Mr. Stedman's suggestion. Perhaps she was thinking of a letter from Mr. Emerson, in which he had written of the necessity for the artist to speak to living man, to speak of a world that was relevant to him in the present. Or perhaps she was genuinely experiencing new emotions and gathering strength. More than likely, all of these played a role in Emma's embarking on a long and ambitious work, *The Dance to Death*. It was a verse drama in five acts, based on authentic historical records of the plague in Europe and the condemnation and death of the Jews in a town in Germany.

Emma set her scene in the small province of Thuringia in the city of Nordhausen. The year is 1349. The Jews who live in a ghetto district are gathering at the synagogue. A visitor, an elderly rabbi, brings news of the epidemic plague and confirms the rumors that Jews are being blamed and buried alive.

> Everywhere torture, smoking Synagogues,
> Carnage and burning flesh. The lights shine out
> Of Jewish virtue, Jewish truth, to star
> The sanguine field with an immortal blazon

Nordhausen, he warns, "shall be swept off from earth." Some cry out, but others shake their heads in disbelief at such horror. Susskind, a noble and respected Jew, assures the synagogue members that they are safe, that they have nothing to fear.

But disquieting news continues to be heard, and the shouts outside the ghetto district grow louder.

> . . . Death to the Jews!
> . . . Their homes shall be,
> A wilderness—drown them in their own blood!

And then the blow is struck! The Nordhausen city officials assemble, and the clerk reads an edict condemning all Jews to be burned to death.

Susskind pleads for mercy.

> We know the Black Death is a scourge of God.
> Is not our flesh as capable of pain,
> Our blood as quick envenomed as your own? . . .
> We drink the waters which our enemies say
> We spoil with poison,—we must breathe, as ye,
> The universal air,—we droop, faint, sicken,
> From the same causes. . . .

But Susskind's words are not heard. The entire locked and guarded ghetto, with no means of escape, is given until sundown to live. The distraught man returns home with the burden of telling his children their fate. "Nerve your young hearts," he says and tries to offer them comfort with the reminder that they will be leaving a world of evil, trouble, and fear.

The condemned begin to make their way toward the synagogue. An old man calls out, asking if his bones have been spared for his life to come to such an end. A young girl cries, "I am too young to die."

Then Susskind delivers a final impassioned speech to his people, telling them that they will die in honor and that from their death shall bloom heroic lives.

> Ours is the truth,
> Ours is the power, the gift of Heaven. We hold
> His Law, His lamp, His covenant, His pledge.
> Wherever in the ages shall arise
> Jew-priest, Jew-poet, Jew-singer, or Jew-saint—
> And everywhere I see them star the gloom—
> In each of these the martyrs are avenged!

Now the sun sets; the bonfire burns. The Jews are dressed in their finest, "dancing in the crimson blaze," bravely meeting their martyrs' deaths. And then they are engulfed by flames, and they perish.

In her poetry Emma said that people perish but the truth survives.

A more powerful and more universal poetic work Emma had never written. What strength of character and substance of theme she had used! What economy and vitality of language! What a difference from her early verse!

Emma had come to realize something vital for an artist. "Wherever there is humanity, there is a theme."

9
Shocking Events

While Emma was writing *The Dance to Death*, a drama set in the fourteenth century, history, five hundred years later, was about to repeat itself. Emma knew nothing of it. Auguste and his French compatriots knew nothing of it. But these new events taking place in the world were to forever change Emma Lazarus, her work, and her life.

The sky grew dark and a storm gathered over the distant lands of Russia, Romania, and Poland, then spread into other areas of Eastern Europe. It was a rage of anti-Semitism so violent that for a long time the world would not comprehend its reality.

It began in Russia in 1881, when the country was ruled by Czar Alexander II. During his reign, he had been good to the Jews in comparison to treatment by other czars. Certainly the Jews were not allowed to come and go as they pleased. They were still forced to live in ghettos—three million were confined to one area called the Pale of Settlement, near Russia's western border. But under Alexander's rule, many children were allowed to attend Russian schools. Alexander even relaxed earlier laws that sent young boys into the czar's army for twenty-five years.

Alexander II was also known for liberating Russia's forty million serfs, following centuries of the brutal system of serfdom. He did not do this because he was a humanitarian, however, but because economic and political changes had pressured him into such an action. But the newly freed serfs were left poor and miserable, with no hope of improving their lot. The nobility and landlords now lived in constant fear of peasant uprisings against them and the czar.

One Sunday in March of 1881, Alexander II was traveling in his carriage, from the Winter Palace in Saint Petersburg to the riding academy. Suddenly a bomb was thrown at the carriage. The czar escaped injury, but he took a step out the door to see what had happened, and a second bomb exploded. This time he was hit, and he fell to the ground in a cloud of smoke. A few hours later the czar was dead.

The revolutionaries, fed up with troubles in their country, had gotten rid of a strong leader. Alexander III came to the throne next, but he was weak and under the rule of the aristocracy. The aristocracy enjoyed its position of power and did everything to hold on to it. What could be done to avoid a revolution?

One good way was to find a scapegoat to confuse the common people and make them believe that something else, not the despotic czar and thieving government, was the cause of their misery. Who was a good scapegoat? The Jews.

Since the Jews weren't allowed to own land, they had become tradesmen, businessmen, and moneylenders. It would not be difficult to make it appear as if they were controlling most of the money and therefore were the reason for the country's economic hardship.

In the town of Elisavetgrad, as the story goes, a drunken peasant and a Jewish innkeeper became embroiled in an argument. Finally they came to blows, and before long, men were attacking Jews inside and outside the inn. Several were badly injured. Elisavetgrad became the model for the village bloodbath.

The riots spread quickly to nearby villages, and then into surrounding provinces, as homes and synagogues were set on fire. Soon Russian cossacks—soldiers—came riding through town after town, terrifying, injuring, and killing Jews. These organized attacks became known as *pogroms*— a Russian word meaning devastation or destruction. Dread lived in the hearts of Jews everywhere.

The Yiddish writer Sholom Aleichem wrote that he recalled hearing rumors that orders were given to attack Jews, but when he and his family saw soldiers coming down the streets, they felt assured at first. "And they did help," he wrote, "but not us. They helped to rob, to beat, to ravish, to despoil. Before our eyes and in the eyes of the whole world, they helped to smash windows, break down doors. . . . They beat Jews grievously—men, women and children—and they shouted, 'Money, give us your money.' Before our eyes women were hurled from windows and children thrown to the cobblestones."

These pogroms were only a foreshadowing of events to come. Next there came the Jewish Question and its solution. The plan was to coerce one-third of the Jews to become baptized, another third were to be expelled from their homeland, and the last third were to be killed. Systematic persecution had begun.

Slowly reports were beginning to appear in newspapers abroad. The London *Times* wrote: "These persecutions, these oppressions, these cruelties, these outrages have taken every form of atrocity in the experience of mankind, or which the resources of the human tongue can describe. Men have been cruelly murdered, women brutally outraged, children dashed to pieces or burnt alive in their homes."

A new newspaper in New York, *The American Hebrew*, also

began to print some reports, but it did not have information of the wide sweep of devastation. Rather, news trickled in bit by bit to the American reader. Emma had become acquainted with the newspaper's editor, Philip Cowen, and she and her family read these small reports. But for a while, like most people, they shut their eyes and ears to the facts. Who could believe such things were actually happening?

By the end of the summer of 1881, the Russian Jews thought that surely the terrible outrages against them would pass. But they did not. In general, life had not been easy or comfortable in the poor, crowded ghetto homes in the first place, but with more pogroms, how could it be worse?

What could the Jews do? Where could they go to escape? Some discussed the idea of a homeland for the Jewish people, who were not wanted anywhere—a return to Palestine—but that was no more than an idea, a Garden of Eden to dream about.

Others talked of America, the place where the "streets were paved with gold," and the schools and the schoolbooks were free, and there was no such thing as a czar. Spirits soared at the thought, although people knew of the hardship of saving money for tickets, the long travel by land to the boats, and the difficult journey by sea. They worried, too, about the problem of remaining religious in a new land that might corrupt them.

But they went. Thousands and thousands of victims of injustice and oppression abandoned their homes, sold the few belongings they owned, and were swept up in the exodus. They flocked to American shores, seeking a new home and a new life.

One group made an appeal: "Give us a chance in your great and glorious land of liberty, whose broad and trackless acres offer an asylum and a place for weary hearts but courageous souls willing to toil and by the sweat of the brow earn our daily bread. . . . With our freedom we shall become new-created for the great struggle."

And a struggle it was for every immigrant, whether a
worker, a tradesman, an intellectual, a mother, or a child.
They came in small groups at first and within a year the boats
were overflowing. By 1924, there was to be a count of more
than four million Jews leaving Eastern Europe, with three
million of those emigrating to the United States.

The ocean crossing was only the beginning, and usually
not a pleasant one. Passengers huddled together in steerage
like cattle. The smells were sickening, the food and water
limited, and privacy impossible. Many became ill; many died.

To come to live in the United States, millions of people braved
an ocean voyage that was full of hardship and danger.   NATIONAL PARK SERVICE: STATUE OF LIBERTY NA-
TIONAL MONUMENT

A young boy who grew up to be a writer told the long story of his immigration and adjustment to the new land in an autobiography entitled *The Education of Abraham Cahan*. Amidst the foul and dismal conditions in steerage, he experienced uplifting moments too. "Evenings were filled with magic hues of sunsets," he wrote. "But as the wonderful colors sank with the sun, our hearts would fill with a terrible longing for home. Then we would draw together and sing our Russian folk songs filled with nostalgia and yearning."

And then after two weeks at sea, the boats pulled into New York Harbor.

In a Yiddish newspaper, the *Jewish Daily Forward*, Cahan wrote: "The immigrant never forgets his entry into a country which is, to him, a new world in the profoundest sense of the term. . . . I conjure up the gorgeousness of the spectacle as it appeared to me on that clear June morning: the magnificent verdure of Staten Island, the tender blue of sea and sky, the dignified bustle of passing craft. . . . I was in a trance. . . . 'This, then is America!' I exclaimed."

From the ships the immigrants were ferried to Castle Garden. A young Russian Jew, I. Kopeloff, described it as an arsenal that struck him with heavy gloom. "It was often so crowded, so jammed, that there was simply nowhere to sit by day, or anyplace to lie down at night—not even on the bare floor.

"The filth was unendurable, so many packages, pillows, feather beds, and foul clothing (often just plain rags) that each immigrant had dragged with him over the seas and clung to as if they were precious—all of this provided great opportunity for vermin, those filthy little beasts, that crawled about freely and openly over the clutter and made life disagreeable."

The sudden and tremendous influx of refugees swamped not only Castle Garden but all temporary housing stations, including the largest one, Ward's Island in the East River.

Hordes of immigrants land at Castle Garden.   NATIONAL
PARK SERVICE: STATUE OF LIBERTY NATIONAL MONUMENT

The sudden wave of incoming people, the confusion caused
by separated families and by hasty medical examinations
simply baffled and overwhelmed New York authorities.

Where were the exiled to go and what were they to do?
How could they learn the language, find a place to live, secure a job?

Clearly a great deal of help was needed. Committees con-
sisting of members from all religious and ethnic backgrounds were formed. Outrage was expressed at the persecutions and murders that were taking place day after day,

and sympathy poured forth for the victims. Of course, there were some people who worried about allowing too many immigrants into the country, and many objected outright. The time was to come, some forty years later, when laws restricting immigration were passed, but for the time being, the lost and frightened refugees needed caring.

Large meetings were held throughout New York. One took place at Chickering Hall. An important speaker that night was former secretary of state William M. Evarts. He was soon to meet and join in committee work with Emma Lazarus.

The community rose to the cause with groups such as the United Hebrew Charities, the Russian Emigrant Relief Fund Committee, the Hebrew Free School Association, and the Ladies Benevolent Society of the Congregation Gates of Prayer. There were also twenty-six New York City synagogues that helped the refugees.

One of the largest and most active organizations was the newly formed Hebrew Emigrant Aid Society, which established an office across the street from Castle Garden and lodging quarters a few blocks away. *The American Hebrew* reported that everyone in the society "devoted themselves wholeheartedly" to the cause, often neglecting their businesses.

Emma's acquaintance, Dr. Gustav Gottheil, was active with the organization, and one day he brought her and some other women to visit Ward's Island to see firsthand, as he described it, "the wretched fugitives . . . the victims of Russian barbarity . . .

"We saw men and women grouped together," Dr. Gottheil wrote, "the little children crouching around them. Beautiful maidens, often in rags, chatted or sat dreamily in corners, their thoughts far away, perhaps with dear ones dragging out their lives in the horrors of Siberia."

Emma, who had always led a refined and sheltered life, had never seen anything like what she witnessed that day at Ward's Island. Dr. Gottheil long remembered how "Emma Lazarus sat gazing at all this. I saw her face, now aglow with

scorn, now suffused with compassion." For the first time she
was brought face-to-face with the results of intolerance and
hatred. How shocked and profoundly moved she was! Only
a short time before she had heard William Evarts, a Christian, speak out in the name of humanity, saying, "It is
oppression of men and women by men and women, and
we are men and women."

Emma's sister Josephine said that Emma's first visit to
Ward's Island and the meaning of William Evart's words were
"a trumpet call that awoke slumbering and unguessed
echoes."

Her verse was to ring out "as it had never rung before—
a clarion note, calling a people to heroic action and unity,
to the consciousness and fulfillment of a grand destiny." She
would soon write "The Banner of the Jew."

> Then from the stony peak there rang
>   A blast to ope the graves: down poured
> The Maccabean clan, who sang
>   Their battle-anthem to the Lord.
> Five heroes lead, and following, see,
>   Ten thousand rush to victory!
>
> Oh for Jerusalem's trumpet now,
>   To blow a blast of shattering power,
> To wake the sleepers high and low,
>   And rouse them to the urgent hour!
> No hand for vengeance—but to save,
>   A million naked swords should wave.

In the last stanzas, the poet expresses thoughts on remaining strong and on the importance of the brave forever
honoring one another.

After that day, Emma visited the immigrants often, both
at Ward's Island and in their new living quarters. She brought
them food and clothing and warm understanding. When she
came to know some of them, she was surprised to learn that

they were not all from the working class. Many were intellectuals, philosophers, and writers. "They were men of brilliant talents and accomplishments," she wrote, "the graduates of Russian universities; scholars of Greek as well as Hebrew, and familiar with all the principal European tongues—engaged in menial drudgery and burning with zeal in the cause of their religious co-religionists."

She felt a strong connection to those people with intelligent and active minds, who were stifled, groping in the dark. Had not she too often felt stifled and unfulfilled? Her friend Rose Hawthorne Lathrop had said it was easy to see how often Emma's gifted mind was "pathetically unsatisfied."

But now Emma had a new voice, a new purpose and meaning. She had nourishment for her mind and her heart. Emma was speaking for the persecuted Jew. She was helping the refugees with money and sincere caring, but what better way for her to speak for unliberated humanity than with the power of her pen.

"I am all Israel's now," Emma said. "Till that cloud pass, I have no thought, no passion, no desire save for my own people."

10
New Light, New Courage

With fervor, Emma flung herself into a life that was more active and more satisfying than any she had ever known. She found both an abounding energy to work for the immigrants and an inner fire to write about their plight with sympathy and compassion.

Her direct aid to the refugees, however, didn't mean that she entered into their world, for they usually lived in densely populated sections without adequate sanitary facilities, were used as cheap labor, struggled with a new language and customs, and often suffered from culture shock and gnawing loneliness. Emma was still the genteel and proper lady who lived uptown, away from the Lower East Side slums with their street peddlers and pushcarts, selling everything and anything, from damaged eggs to used eyeglasses.

Abraham Cahan remembered meeting Emma shortly after he arrived. She was a "wealthy young Jewish lady who belonged to the cream of monied aristocracy," he wrote. "She

Homeless immigrant children sleeping in the Mulberry Street area of New York City   JACOB A. RIIS COLLECTION/MUSEUM OF THE CITY OF NEW YORK

Hester Street pushcart market on the Lower East Side of New York   THE BYRON COLLECTION/MUSEUM OF THE CITY OF NEW YORK

often visited the immigrants' camp on Ward's Island, but this never undermined her status as an aristocrat." Philip Cowen remembered her once wondering out loud what her society friends would say if they saw her in such "unsavory surroundings."

But whereas it was not in her upbringing or her nature to belittle her status, she felt an abiding sympathy toward the victims she now called her brothers and sisters, and joined committee after committee to arrange for practical and useful help for them. After all, they needed proper housing facilities and schools to learn not only English but useful skills that could provide them with a livelihood.

Morever, Emma was overcoming her shyness. Her sincere and genuine need to relieve the refugees' overwhelming problems allowed her to open up and speak comfortably among her committee friends. James Hoffman, who became president of a technical school for boys, said Emma had "deep insight into the needs and wants of our people," and the way she expressed herself left a lasting impression on him. Emma began spending long and arduous hours in committee planning and began contributing money to the refugees as well. She took a particular interest in the education of a young medical student, known as Mr. Finkelstein, from Odessa, Russia, who, in addition to his studies, was teaching seventy fellow newcomers the fundamentals of the English language.

Another concern of Emma's was improving the wretched living conditions for those on Ward's Island. Men, women, and children were packed into temporary buildings, no better than animals in a stockyard. Furthermore, Emma foresaw the problems growing worse as the winter approached, and there would be no way to provide heat.

In an effort to call attention to the need for new living quarters, she described in a letter to *The American Hebrew* the deplorable situation she saw: "The only appliances for washing consist of about a dozen tubs in the laundry and ten bath-tubs in the lavatory. Not a drop of running water is to be found in dormitories or refectories, or in any of the other buildings, except the kitchen. In all weather, those who desire to wash their hands or to fetch a cup of water, have to walk over several hundred feet of irregular, dirty ground, strewn with rubbish and refuse, and filled, after a rainfall, with stagnant pools of muddy water in which throngs of idle children are allowed to dabble at will."

It was clear to Emma that a program of physical improvement was hardly enough to solve the situation endured by the refugees who were arriving day after day. That first year of the wave of Eastern European immigration, seven hundred thousand passed through the portals of Castle Garden. They had to be settled. They had to find work. Emma recognized the pressing need to begin a program of education and manual training, so she called a meeting of several people devoted to the cause. One was her friend Philip Cowen of *The American Hebrew*, who, with another committee member, took a trip to Boston and Philadelphia to study the methods of their industrial schools.

In time, as a result of Emma's urging, the Hebrew Technical Institute was founded, making use of two complete stories of a spacious building on Crosby Street. There, teenage boys learned the use of tools and, so that their general education should not be neglected, as reported in *The American Hebrew*, there was instruction in English and oral communication "to make the boys think for themselves."

As occupied as Emma was with committee work and with helping her new brothers and sisters, her bright light came from her pen.

Of Emma, Philip Cowen wrote, "When public-spirited Jews and Christians concerned themselves with the future of the refugees, Emma was in the forefront of those Americans who endeavored to help." He sought her poetry and other writings to publish in *The American Hebrew*, and she became a regular contributor.

In "The Crowing of the Red Cock," Emma asked how Christians could be so destructive and violate God's teachings. She wrote the poem at the time the Russian skies were red with the blaze of Jewish homes and synagogues, and it aroused attention and indignation at the despicable crimes.

One day Mr. Cowen came to pay a call on Emma. Would she write a poem to celebrate the Jewish New Year? he asked.

"I cannot write to order," Emma answered. It was her usual answer when a subject was suggested to her. She felt she could write only out of inspiration, only when her heart moved her to do so. But Mr. Cowen knew Emma. He knew that she wouldn't be able to resist the theme. He was right. A few days later, when he opened his mail he found a poem she had written, a joyous, triumphant celebration called "The New Year Rosh Hashanah 5643" (the Hebrew calendar year for 1882).

Not while the snow-shroud round dead earth is rolled,
    And naked branches point to frozen skies,—
When orchards burn their lamps of fiery gold,
    The grape glows like a jewel, and the corn
A sea of beauty and abundance lies,
        Then the new year is born.

Look where the mother of the months uplifts
    In the green clearness of the unsunned West,
Her ivory horn of plenty, dropping gifts,
    Cool, harvest-feeding dews, fine-winnowed light;
Tired labor with fruition, joy and rest
        Profusely to requite.

Blow, Israel, the sacred cornet! Call
    Back to thy courts whatever faint heart throb
With thine ancestral blood, thy need craves all.
    The red, dark year is dead, the year just born
Leads on from anguish wrought by priest and mob,
        To what undreamed-of morn?

In the last five stanzas, Emma went on to express further thoughts about the new year at the time of crisis in Jewish history. She spoke of two different streams the exiled were following—one to the ancient homeland of Israel and the other to America. But she wrote that they were all embracing the world. At the end she sang out "Rejoice . . . for Truth and Law and Love."

Soon afterward Emma wrote a calmer, more peaceful poem, "In Exile." It was inspired by a letter written by a Russian Jewish refugee living with his family in Texas. He wrote, "Since that day till now our life is one unbroken paradise. We live a true brotherly life. Every evening after supper we take a seat under the mighty oak and sing our songs." Emma had never journeyed west, nor had she even visited a farm or ranch, but she imagined a day on the wide open spaces where "soft breezes bow the grass" and "the broad prairie melts in mist of tears."

The letter had been shown to Emma by a friend whom she had met through her committee work, a man who had also been persuaded to visit Ward's Island. His name was Michael Heilprin, and he was an immigrant who had years earlier fled Poland for Hungary to escape Polish oppression. Then, in 1856, at the age of thirty-three, he had set out for the United States. He was well educated and spoke twelve languages. When Emma met him, he was working on the *New American Cyclopaedia*. His house was described by his friends as a "library and a literary workshop."

Like Emma, he began to devote himself to aiding the immigrants. When his own pockets were emptied, he went to others to plead for the immigrants' cause. He was so sensitive to the immigrants' pride in not wanting to ask for financial help that once he invented a job for a man so the man wouldn't feel he was receiving charity. Mr. Heilprin hired him as a secretary when there was really no work for a secretary to do.

Mr. Heilprin proved to be a sympathetic and supportive

friend. He often accompanied Emma to meetings. Many of these gatherings were held at the home of their mutual companion, Dr. Gustav Gottheil. Years earlier when Dr. Gottheil had asked her to write original hymns with a Jewish theme, Emma had refused. But now she was in the midst of a rich outpouring of Jewish verse.

She was aiming not only to arouse indignation at injustice and persecution but also to continually emphasize the need for sympathy and understanding of the victims. Tucked away in Emma's drawer was a work she had written earlier, and she took it out to look at again. It was the verse drama *The Dance to Death.* What a perfect drama to arouse sympathy, she realized. And then an idea came to her. Why not ask Mr. Cowen to print it in a special inexpensive pamphlet form so that it would be easily available to a large audience? The publisher was enthusiastic. In discussing the pamphlet, they came up with another idea. Why not print the drama along with several of Emma's Jewish poems? That would lend the publication additional strength. The title they settled upon was *Songs of a Semite.* Without delay, Emma and Mr. Cowen went to work on the publication. The selling price was twenty-five cents, and as Emma hoped, it became a popular edition and caused the intended emotional response among the readers.

Emma's new work had brought her new friends and renewed old friendships as well. It was good to be sharing common concerns and feelings with other people. "I thank you most earnestly," Emma wrote Dr. Gottheil, "for showing me the way and inspiring me with the courage to carry out my own impulse—which without your assistance and cooperation I should never have been able to accomplish."

Now Emma had a favor to ask of him. She wanted to learn the Hebrew language. As soon as Dr. Gottheil helped her find a tutor, she eagerly undertook the studies. The tutor was Louis Schnabel, superintendent of the Hebrew Orphan Asylum. He was followed by another teacher, Professor Arnold Ehrlich, an instructor at the Emanu-El Preparatory School.

Emma progressed so quickly with her lessons that within the year she was able to begin translating Hebrew poets from their original script. One day Mr. Cowen received an envelope containing a poem of a medieval Spanish Hebrew poet, along with a note from Emma. "I have translated this from the original Hebrew—and so am very proud of it as my first effort!"

Sometimes Emma mailed her work to Mr. Cowen; at other

Emma's first translation of a Hebrew poem for *The American Hebrew*   AMERICAN JEWISH HISTORICAL SOCIETY times she delivered it in person. In his autobiography, *Memories of an American Jew*, Philip Cowen wrote a brief account of one of her visits. She liked the atmosphere of the printing office, he said, and she came to see him at odd times because she knew he was busy during regular office hours. "I shall never forget one such visit," he wrote. "I had taken down a printing press to clean. I looked like a dozen printers' devils rolled into one. Old clothes, hands and face black with smudge, I felt rather uncomfortable. But Miss Lazarus refused to hear my apology, saying that if she broke in on me at such an inopportune time, she was the one who should apologize."

The poet then insisted the publisher continue his work, and she set a typecase on end, perched herself on it, and told him the reason for her visit. It was to collect more money for the young medical student, Mr. Finkelstein.

Richard Watson Gilder was a man who had long been a friend of the Lazarus family, but now Emma became an even closer friend and colleague of his. He was a poet, essayist, and editor of the magazine the *Century*, formerly called *Scribner's Monthly*, which had published several of Emma's early poems.

The April 1882 edition of the *Century* was an important issue for Emma for two reasons. First, there appeared in it an article she had written several months earlier. It was an article discussing the difficult circumstances under which the Jewish religion had been preserved throughout the centuries. What did she conclude in this discussion? Judaism had been deprived of natural development, she said, and the test of the survival of the Jewish people would be in the next hundred years.

When the issue arrived at her house, after she looked at her article, she thumbed through the other pages. There appeared an article by a woman named Madame Zinaida Alexievna Ragozin, a historian and member of European society. At first glance Emma saw that Madame Ragozin had analyzed the pogroms "from a Russian point of view." Then as she read on, she realized the writer was actually defending the pogroms. Emma was shocked!

Madame Ragozin wrote that while some Jews saw God, others worshiped the Golden Calf. Those who worshiped money and gold, she said, robbed the Gentiles, and when the Gentiles fought back, the Jews would not stand up for themselves because money was more important than their honor. What was Madame Ragozin's solution? Let the Jews be forbidden to be Jews.

Choked with rage, Emma hurried to Mr. Gilder and asked how he could print such an article. Of course, he disagreed with the author, but he explained that as a journalist, sometimes it was necessary to print a different viewpoint, no matter how unpopular or controversial.

Understanding Mr. Gilder, but enraged at what Madame Ragozin had to say, Emma responded in the next month's issue. She went to Mr. Heilprin for help and replied with intelligent, convincing arguments. She said the Jews in Russia were denied the protection of the law, so how could they stand up for themselves? Furthermore, she answered the charge that there were two kinds of Jews by saying "the dualism of Jews is the dualism of humanity." There are good and bad in everyone. Emma's reply was a resounding protest. Never had she spoken so clearly and so distinctly.

Emma began to find that she had so much to say, she couldn't express it all in poetry or essays. Even though she had overcome her shyness when she spoke at committee meetings, she would never stand up and speak publicly. A new idea came to her. She would write a series of letters for *The American Hebrew.* She called them "An Epistle to the Hebrews."

The series demonstrated a burst of creative energy and allowed her to expound on any number of subjects. Her main concern was that Jews were suffering from increasing anti-

Semitism—from accusations of thirsting for money and also of binding themselves together too closely. She insisted that Jews thirsted not for money but for knowledge and truth. Through her letters, she hoped to give Jews a sense of pride.

In one letter she called for a bridge to be built between the past and the future, so there would be a "closer union and warmer patriotism" among Jews in America. In another she argued that contrary to belief, Jews were both capable of working and willing to work in the fields of agriculture. In still another she urged that all men and women reach out to give aid to the helpless.

Some of the letters were controversial and caused a debate among the readers. Years before work began toward the building of a national Jewish homeland in Palestine, Emma spoke out for its establishment. She also wrote that the Sabbath should not be a day of piety and repentance, but one of joy. And she even went so far as to say that for surviving in the world, industrial education was more important for Jewish boys than any other kind of education, including the study of the sacred Torah!

More than once Emma was attacked for her views, both in print and face-to-face. Most people, though, admired her. Dr. Abram Isaacs, editor of the *Jewish Messenger*, wrote in his newspaper that he approved the "bold and courageous manner in which she championed the Jews."

Emma, the modest and soft-spoken woman, the romantic poet of yesteryear, had indeed become bold and courageous. What a long and winding road she had traveled.

11
Inspiration

Emma had never worked so hard and with such zeal. After two years with little rest, she found herself exhausted. Friends suggested a trip abroad. Although she had read about Europe and had long been reading the great European writers, she had never seriously considered travel.

If ever she were to visit the charming old world she had for years envisioned, what better time than the present? It would be a good change for her. Besides, she wanted to meet with Europe's leading Jewish and intellectual figures to gain their sympathy and help for her cause. Mr. Cowen, Dr. Gottheil, and Michael Heilprin all gave her letters of introduction to important people, just as Edouard Laboulaye had done with Auguste for his first journey across the Atlantic. In the nineteenth century, that was the proper way for a member of society to make a new acquaintance.

On May 15, 1883, Emma and her younger sister Annie sailed on the S.S. *Alaska* for England. It was a lovely, relaxing trip. Each day, ships carrying Europeans passed on their way to the new land. Auguste had beautifully recorded his impressions of ocean travel and his arrival in America. Now Emma was writing her impressions about the sea, "a vision of beauty from morning till night . . . the sea like a mirror and the sky dazzling with light." And she wrote of her excitement at reaching her destination, "An hour or two before sunset came the great sensation of—land! At first, nothing but a shadow on the far horizon, like the ghost of a ship."

In England she was dazed with the novelty and charm. "I drink in, at every sense, the sights, sounds, and smells, and the unimaginable beauty of it all," she wrote. With her sister, she was graciously received and entertained by those who read the letters of introduction she carried from her friends at home. There was one person in particular she hoped to meet, if only for a few minutes, and their meeting went beyond Emma's expectations. It was the poet Robert Browning. He sent a note to her hotel, inviting her to his home for tea. For Emma, long an admirer of him and his deceased wife, the poet Elizabeth Barrett Browning, it was an extraordinary afternoon.

After England, Emma traveled to France, but she found the country "disquieting," and Paris a city "seared with fire and blood" after so long a history of turmoil. While in Paris, did she see the Statue of Liberty towering above the city from its courtyard studio? Perhaps she did. And perhaps, witnessing firsthand a country that had long suffered tyranny, her already fervent feelings for mankind's liberty were deepened. "Until we are all free," she wrote, "we are none of us free."

By the time Emma returned home, the continuing confusion and clamor over the pedestal for the statue had reached a peak. The statue was nearly ready to be sent, but America was not ready to receive it. There was still too little money for the pedestal, and worse, there was even less enthusiasm.

The pedestal had been designed and planned by the architect Richard Morris Hunt. He and Auguste had met during Auguste's first trip to New York, and they found much in common to discuss. Richard had attended a school of fine arts in Paris. Casually Auguste had asked him how he would like to build a pedestal for the world's largest statue. Richard smiled and agreed without hesitation. But he had thought Auguste was joking and was surprised to learn that the French sculptor was serious. Still intrigued, though, the architect said he would be delighted to do the job.

Of course, years had gone by, and now there was only enough money to excavate a foundation and no more. Richard Morris Hunt had designed dozens of mansions for New York and Newport millionaires, but none of his clients were willing to contribute. Not even *The New York Times*, pointing out that the "French committee feels somewhat hurt by our tardiness," could succeed in moving the wealthy to send a small sum.

The American committee went to the government to ask for an appropriation, but after days of bickering, the answer was no. It seemed there might never be a pedestal. What a terrible and insulting situation for the French! The committee didn't know where to turn.

At last one man rose to the forefront to make the difference. He was an immigrant from Hungary who had come during the Civil War to fight on the side of the Union. This man was now a successful newspaper publisher by the name of Joseph Pulitzer, the journalist who established the annually awarded Pulitzer prizes. With his newspaper, the New York *World*, and the power of the press, he started a dramatic campaign. "New York ought to blush at this humiliating spectacle," he wrote. "The statue, the noble gift of our young sister republic is ready for us . . . and we stand haggling and begging and scheming in order to raise enough money."

Day after day Joseph Pulitzer printed pleas, and the money began to trickle in. It came from people all over the United

States. "I am only a sewing girl, but I am in full sympathy with your effort," a girl who signed her letter Jane M. wrote, and enclosed fifty cents. "I work for a living, but I can afford a dollar for the cause," wrote John Bolton. A Union soldier collected money in a saloon from two Germans, four Americans, and three Irishmen, "all patriots in a small way," the soldier explained.

A child scrawled, "I am a wee bit of a girl, yet I am ever so glad that I was born in a time to contribute. . . . When I am old enough, I will ask my Mama and Papa to take me to see the statue, and I will always be proud that I began my career by sending you one dollar to aid in so good a cause."

Now all of America was becoming part of the campaign. Work on the pedestal began again, but once more, money ran out. One final push was needed to reach the goal. This time the pedestal fund committee decided to hold an art-loan exhibition and fund-raising auction. Famous artists would submit their work for display, and writers would submit works to be published in a portfolio to go on the auction block. The list of writers was impressive. It included the humorist Mark Twain, the poet Walt Whitman, and the naturalist John Burroughs, who was a friend of Emma's. Also, well-known stage actors and actresses were offering autographs.

Since Emma was an important and well-known poet, Senator William Evarts, chairman of the exhibit, wanted her to be included in the portfolio. Not long after she returned from Europe, he approached her and asked if she would contribute a poem or essay she had written.

"No, I have nothing I consider appropriate," she answered.

"Then will you write something special for the occasion?" he asked.

"Oh, no, that won't be possible at all," Emma said. "I cannot write to order."

Dismayed, Senator Evarts gave up. But immediately afterward, another committee member paid a visit to Emma. Her name was Constance Cary Harrison. She was in charge of compiling the portfolio. Emma was polite to Mrs. Harrison, but insisted that if she attempted to write to order, "under the circumstances, it will assuredly be flat."

What was left but for Mrs. Harrison to appeal to Emma's emotions? She told her to think of the statue holding her torch out to the Russian refugees, so lost and frightened, yet so full of hope. "The shaft sped home," Mrs. Harrison recalled of Emma. "Her dark eyes deepened—her cheek flushed . . . she said not a word more."

Soon afterward Emma began work on a poem. It was a sonnet, a fourteen-line poem with a particular rhyme and meter. This one she called "1492," and in it she wrote about two events that happened that year—the expulsion of the Jews from Spain and Spain's sending explorer Christopher Columbus westward to open doors to a new land. In the sonnet Emma called 1492 a "two-faced year." But she wasn't satisfied with it as a submission.

She sat down to try a second poem, which she entitled "Gifts." In it she spoke of the Egyptians seeking wealth, the Greeks seeking beauty, the Romans seeking power, and the Hebrews seeking truth. The Hebrew, she wrote, had throughout history been exiled from his home, but still he remained searching, a "lamp within his hand."

Then Emma pictured the image of a lamplight leading the way to justice and truth. She thought of the Colossus of Rhodes, a huge bronze statue of the sun god, Helios, built in a Greek harbor in ancient days, later destroyed by an earthquake. Now America would have a monument at its gateway, and a small contribution from her pen could help place it there to welcome the refugees she so cared for.

Truly inspired at last, Emma sat down and once more wrote. This sonnet she called "The New Colossus."

Not like the brazen giant of Greek fame,
With conquering limbs astride from land to land;
Here at our sea-washed, sunset gates shall stand
A mighty woman with a torch, whose flame
Is the imprisoned lightning, and her name
Mother of Exiles. From her beacon-hand
Glows world-wide welcome; her mild eyes command
The air-bridged harbor that twin cities frame.
"Keep, ancient lands, your storied pomp!" cries she
With silent lips. "Give me your tired, your poor,
Your huddled masses yearning to breathe free,
The wretched refuse of your teeming shore.
Send these, the homeless, tempest-tost to me,
I lift my lamp beside the golden door!"

At the bottom she added the words *Written in aid of Bartholdi Pedestal Fund 1883* and sent the sonnet to the committee.

Mrs. Harrison called it "a welcomed treasure."

The exhibit opened in December at the National Academy of Design on Fourth Avenue. The verses in the collection were read aloud, and the portfolio went for $1,500 to the highest bidder, a man named Lydig Suydam. The exhibit ran for four weeks and raised enough money to see the pedestal through its completion.

Meanwhile, Emma received an unexpected letter. It was from James Russell Lowell, a poet and critic, who at the time was the American envoy to England. "I like your sonnet about the Statue," he wrote. "Much better than I like the Statue itself. But your sonnet gives its subject a *raison d'etre* [reason to be] which it wanted before quite as much as it wants a pedestal. You have set it on a noble one, saying admirably just the right word to be said, an achievement more arduous than that of the sculptor."

Emma was thrilled to receive the letter, except she gave little further thought to the sonnet or the statue. But Mr. Lowell's message was prophetic. It seemed to whisper words of something to come true in the future.

Manuscript of "The New Colossus," the sonnet written to raise money for the completion of the Statue of Liberty's pedestal   MUSEUM OF THE CITY OF NEW YORK

For now, though, the owner of the portfolio simply took it home. It would still be many years before anyone besides Mr. Lowell would recognize how worthy was the noble and moving sonnet Emma had written.

12
A Stilled Voice

In France the huge sections of the statue were packed into two hundred and fourteen immense crates. Each dismantled piece was marked and numbered so that the giant jigsaw puzzle could be reassembled. The packing had taken a total of seventeen days. Seventy railway cars had transported the crates from Paris one hundred and thirty-nine miles away to the river port in Rouen.

Auguste and Jeanne-Emilie stood on the shore and watched the last of the cases loaded onto the steamship *Isère*. Imagine how Auguste felt, spending all those years creating such a work of art and then having to part with it.

It was a gray, drizzly day, but he hardly noticed. He was too full of emotion. He was experiencing a heightened sense of pride and accomplishment, yet he also felt sad and empty as the whistle blew and the ship moved out, heading toward the Atlantic Ocean. For one, his friend Edouard Laboulaye had not lived to see this glorious occasion. He had died two years earlier. For another, as Auguste watched the ship disappear, he seemed to be watching part of himself leave too.

"Goodbye, my daughter, Liberty," he whispered. "At last you are going home."

It was May 22, 1885, and France's extraordinary gift was actually on its way to America. *Isère* and its treasured cargo arrived in New York on June 17.

The pedestal was nearing completion. It rested within the star-shaped walls of Fort Wood, which had been built in the first half of the nineteenth century as part of the defense

Construction of the pedestal of the Statue of Liberty was funded by contributions from people of all ages and from all walks of life.   NATIONAL PARK SERVICE: STATUE OF LIBERTY NATIONAL MONUMENT

against naval attack in New York Harbor. Richard Morris
Hunt's one hundred and forty-nine-foot pedestal had taken
on strength and grandeur. Both the architect and the sculptor had been right in planning a pedestal that would so
magnificently balance the monument.

Then, at last, the pedestal was ready. The enormous and
difficult task of reassembling the statue and affixing it to the
pedestal began. Inside the pedestal two sets of massive steel
beams were locked into the steel skeleton as the frame was
raised. So firmly were they locked together, it was said, that
to topple the structure, the entire Bedloe's Island would have
to be turned upside down.

Piece by piece the giant jigsaw puzzle was reconstructed,
and on October 28, 1886, Liberty Enlightening the World was
unveiled and dedicated. What a truly amazing monument it
was! One hundred fifty-one feet of gleaming copper,
weighing two hundred twenty-five tons. There were one
hundred sixty-seven steps inside the pedestal and one
hundred seventy-one in the statue's spiral staircase leading
to the crown.

After so much time, work, and fund-raising, after so much
bickering and haggling, the vision of the Statue of Liberty
had become a reality.

Immediately the statue took on different meanings to different people. For some it signified the intended bond of
friendship between France and America. For others it meant
the victory of democracy over the chains of oppression. Some
even questioned the appropriateness of a nonreligious statue
in the America they viewed as a "Christian country."

Of all the newspapers who wrote about the statue, only
the New York *Herald* commented on its meaning to immigrants. The *Herald* remarked that for those who had struggled to get to the New World, liberty, as represented by the
woman with the torch, was the very air they breathed.

And, of course, there was the contribution of Emma Lazarus. But neither was she present at the dedication cere-

The Statue of Liberty   NATIONAL PARK SERVICE: STATUE OF
LIBERTY NATIONAL MONUMENT

mony, nor was her sonnet read. It remained in the fund-raising portfolio, and no one even knew where the portfolio was at the time.

Emma's beloved father had died the year before. And now she herself was gravely ill. She had traveled to Europe once again, but was so weak she could barely make the return journey.

It was only such a short time ago that she had finally found a sense of identity and a meaning for her life that was both giving and rewarding. She had gained an honorable place among Jews and Christians alike. She was recognized by all who knew her as "a soul dedicated to aiding the oppressed." And now she was suffering from incurable cancer.

A year after the statue was unveiled, her newly found poetic voice was stilled. On November 19, 1887, Emma Lazarus died, and she was buried in the family plot at Beth El Fields in Cypress Hills, New York. Emma was only thirty-eight years old.

13
Her Words Forever Sing

Emma's sonnet might have been completely forgotten if it hadn't been for another woman, an aristocratic and soft-spoken person, much like Emma Lazarus herself. Her name was Georgina Schuyler.

Georgina was a patroness of the arts and also a humanitarian who had spent much of her time during the Civil War aiding soldiers in a New York State hospital.

One day in 1903, she was browsing in a used book shop in New York City, and there, among a pile of dusty old books, she came upon a small portfolio. Curious, she picked it up and casually began thumbing through it. One poem struck her at once. It was "The New Colossus."

How touching the words and images were to Georgina. How meaningful they would be if linked with the Statue of Liberty, she thought.

Georgina Schuyler purchased the portfolio and hurried from the shop to show it to friends. With an eye for beauty

and a soul for giving art further depth, she then arranged
to have the last five lines of the sonnet engraved on a plaque.
And that same year, the plaque was placed inside the second story of the statue's pedestal.

There was no fanfare, no recorded ceremonial date. There
was no mention in a speech or in print of the years of hope
and despair and toil in the lives of the sculptor and the poet.
It just happened by chance that one day a thoughtful woman
added the final piece to the giant jigsaw puzzle in New York
Harbor. On that ordinary day, however, Auguste's monument and Emma's deeply inspired poem were united at last.

In time, people came to recognize the symbol as the Mother

The plaque containing Emma's most famous poem, "The New
Colossus," was placed on the statue's pedestal years after
the statue's completion.   NATIONAL PARK SERVICE: STATUE
OF LIBERTY NATIONAL MONUMENT

of Exiles. Castle Garden and Ward's Island were closed and replaced by a larger and more accommodating immigrant depot station, Ellis Island. But for the "wretched refuse" journeying by sea, their first sight of America was always the awesome one of Liberty Enlightening the World. To them it was a gift of promise, a gift of hope. One immigrant from Yugoslavia, Louis Adamic, became a noted author and during the first half of the new century crusaded endlessly to elevate the position of the immigrant. Whatever he wrote, wherever he spoke, he quoted from "The New Colossus."

Like Emma, Auguste Bartholdi never came to know of the new meaning given to his statue. He died of tuberculosis on October 4, 1904. That was in the midst of a period in Jewish history when a second terrifying sweep of pogroms in Eastern Europe sent a new tide of Jews to America's shores.

In the 1930s, Emma's poem began to receive even further attention when it was included in school textbooks and children everywhere were taught to recite it. It was even put to music by the famous Russian-born American songwriter, Irving Berlin, for a Broadway musical called *Miss Liberty*.

In 1945, when World War II ended, following the devastation of Europe and European Jewry by Nazi barbarism, the pedestal plaque was removed, and the entire sonnet was engraved and placed over the statue's main entrance. There it remains today. In addition, a tablet bearing the last lines of the sonnet also stands at New York's John F. Kennedy International Airport customs entrance, where many immigrants now arrive in the United States. Then, in 1956, the name of Bedloe's Island, as Auguste had once quietly suggested, was officially changed to Liberty Island.

Throughout history, in every field of endeavor, there have been people whose contributions to the world have not been recognized until after their death. Emma was one of those people. Her friends and colleagues wrote glowingly of her in a memorial edition of *The American Hebrew* in December

As most immigrants to the United States now arrive by plane, a portion of "The New Colossus" was engraved on a plaque that stands in John F. Kennedy International Airport in New York. THE PORT OF NEW YORK AUTHORITY

1887. Robert Browning, with whom she shared so much during their time together in England, wired a cablegram, sending "admiration for the genius and love of my lamented friend." Poet John Greenleaf Whittier wrote that "the Semitic race has had no braver singer." John Burroughs, who "felt a personal bereavement in her death," also "valued her

Emma Lazarus Memorial Number.

THE
AMERICAN HEBREW

Vol. 33.—No. 5.   NEW YORK, FRIDAY, KISLEV 23, DECEMBER 9, 5648.   Subscription: $3.00 per annum
Single Copies Ten Cents.

TO MORROW, Saturday night, will be the first night of Chanuka, or Feast of Lights, or Feast of Dedication, the anniversary of the dedication of the Temple of Jerusalem after the successful war of the Maccabees.

IN spite of the twenty pages we have added to THE AMERICAN HEBREW this week, we find it necessary at the last moment to omit our Philadelphia and Baltimore letters, considerable local news and several contributed articles of interest.

THE Critic of this week will also honor the memory of Emma Lazarus. Its leading article will be devoted to her; and an estimate of her life from a Jewish point of view will be given by Dr. Pereira Mendes and there will be a sonnet by Mr. Chas. de Kay. Thanks to authors and publishers, we are enabled to print this sonnet of Mr. de Kay, and also have the pleasure of adding to our other contributors the name of Mr. Cross whose poem reached the Critic too late for use in its current issue.

OUR London brethren are endeavoring to unite the numberless chebras at the East End, and no less personages than F. D. Mocatta and Samuel Montagu, M. P., are actively at work to secure that object. It is not intended that the organizations should in any way yield their autonomy. They are simply to be united for such purposes as are of mutual interest to them, the engagement of competent ministers, the instruction of the young, and to generally improve their condition. It is a movement which we could well imitate in this city and which has been attempted here, but thus far has failed of fruition.

WE have attempted in this issue to do honor to the memory of Emma Lazarus, the "sweet singer in Israel," and to that end invited a number of men and women prominent in the republic of letters, who either knew her personally or through her writings, to join us in our endeavor. It may be that we omitted to invite some who would have been glad to add some tribute to her memory; it may be that some who were asked found the little time given for reply insufficient to adequately express themselves. We therefore, beg to state that we will be pleased to receive further contributions, which we will gather in a subsequent issue of THE AMERICAN HEBREW.

THE question has frequently been asked why the "Songs of a Semite" was published in the somewhat undesirable form in which it appears, as the gems of such a poet as the author deserved a better setting. It is but proper to say that when Miss Lazarus was in negotiation with THE AMERICAN HEBREW for the publication of the "Dance of Death" and the other poems that go to make up the volume, she wrote as follows: "It is my idea to have the pamphlet issued at as low a price and in as simple a form as possible," and she would entertain no proposition to publish the volume in any other form. She wished to give the book a large circulation among those of her people who could not buy costly ones, and in this she succeeded.

WHILE the first flush of wonderment at the marvellous performances by one so young may have warmed the hearts of critical musicians on the first night of Josef Hofmann's appearance at the Metropolitan Opera House, repeated hearings have only intensified the impressions which his mastery of the piano then created. Those who are best capable of forming intelligent opinions on what after all is the interesting technical question involved agree that he possesses more than the mere "infant prodigy" talent for exciting admiration, and is in very truth, a born musician, one with the musical ear and soul, capable of development to the loftiest pitch of human possibilities in the sphere of musical interpretation and perhaps of creation.

IN response to several requests to publish the admirable Thanksgiving address which Prof. Henry M. Leipziger delivered at Temple Beth-El, we print this week a liberal extract. This address is quite in keeping with the previous pulpit efforts of Prof. Leipziger, and displays a power of language which may well excite admiration. One of the correspondents asks why it is that, while other young men from all parts of the country have been invited to speak in Temple Emanu-El, Mr. Leipziger has not been asked, although he is known to be an excellent speaker and a good thinker; he has spoken before several other congregations with excellent effect, and he has been in past years identified with the religious school of the Temple. We can only say that it may be a case of "no man a prophet in his own country." Yet, we would like to hear Prof. Leipziger in this pulpit. He has devoted considerable attention during the last few years to the study of theology and kindred subjects, and he has specially qualified himself to meet those very religious questions which agitate the young men and women of to-day.

Front page of *The American Hebrew* memorial edition for Emma Lazarus, December 9, 1887   AMERICAN JEWISH HISTORICAL SOCIETY

Emma Lazarus   AMERICAN JEWISH ARCHIVES/HEBREW UNION
COLLEGE

not merely for her literary genius . . . but for her sympathy and attraction as a person, her grace and sweetness as a woman."

Emma Lazarus, the Jewish and American poet, was hailed as "a sweet singer of Israel," but her voice sang out for all humanity. And the beacon she held helped to lead the way for others to enter her America and breathe the treasured air of freedom.

Emma, who had longed to accomplish something to awaken the world, has through her poetry forever reminded us that liberty must never be taken for granted. She has indeed awakened us. She has stirred us all.

Books for Further Reading

Burchard, Sue. *The Statue of Liberty: Birth to Rebirth.* New York: Harcourt Brace Jovanovich, 1985.

Fisher, Leonard Everett. *The Statue of Liberty.* New York: Holiday House, 1985.

Harris, Jonathan. *A Statue for America: The First 100 Years of the Statue of Liberty.* New York: Four Winds Press, 1985.

Schappes, Morris U., editor. *Emma Lazarus: Selections From Her Poetry and Prose.* New York: Emma Lazarus Federation of Jewish Women's Clubs, 1982.

Shapiro, Mary J. *How They Built the Statue of Liberty.* New York: Random House, 1985.

Index

Page numbers in *italics* refer to captions.

About the Author

NANCY SMILER LEVINSON has worked as a newspaper reporter, a paperback-books editor, and a teacher in the Head Start program for disadvantaged preschool children. She is the author of many biographies and novels for young adults, including her recently published first hardcover novel, *The Ruthie Greene Show*.

"Emma Lazarus seemed the perfect subject for me," she says. "During Emma's lifetime, short as it was, she changed. She grew to be deeply concerned with the cause of immigration and the importance of freedom, subjects which also touch me profoundly." Mrs. Levinson lives with her husband and two children in southern California.